FINDING
LUBCHENKO

FINDING
LUBCHENKO

Michael Simmons

razOr
bill

Finding Lubchenko

RAZORBILL

Published by the Penguin Group
Penguin Young Readers Group
345 Hudson Street, New York, New York 10014, U.S.A.
Penguin Group (USA) Inc., 375 Hudson Street, New York, New York 10014, U.S.A.
Penguin Books Canada Ltd, 10 Alcorn Avenue, Toronto, Ontario, Canada M4V 3B2
(a division of Pearson Penguin Canada, Inc.)
Penguin Books Ltd, 80 Strand, London WC2R 0RL, England
Penguin Ireland, 25 St Stephen's Green, Dublin 2, Ireland
(a division of Penguin Books Ltd)
Penguin Group (Australia), 250 Camberwell Road, Camberwell, Victoria 3124,
Australia (a division of Pearson Australia Group Pty Ltd)
Penguin Books India Pvt Ltd, 11 Community Centre, Panchsheel Park,
New Delhi – 110 017, India
Penguin Group (NZ), Cnr Airborne and Rosedale Roads, Albany, Auckland 1310,
New Zealand (a division of Pearson New Zealand Ltd)
Penguin Books (South Africa) (Pty) Ltd, 24 Sturdee Avenue, Rosebank,
Johannesburg 2196, South Africa

Penguin Books Ltd, Registered Offices: 80 Strand, London WC2R 0RL, England

10 9 8 7 6 5 4 3 2 1

Copyright 2005 © Michael Simmons
All rights reserved

Interior design by Christopher Grassi

Library of Congress Cataloging-in-Publication Data

Simmons, Michael.
  Finding Lubchenko / by Michael Simmons.
    p. cm.
  Summary: When his father is framed for murder and bioterrorism,
high-school junior Evan, using clues from a stolen laptop, travels from
Seattle to Paris with two friends to find the real culprit.
  ISBN 1-59514-021-2 (hardcover)
  [1. Fathers—Fiction. 2. Murder—Fiction. 3. Bioterrorism—Fiction.
4. Paris (France)—Fiction. 5. Mystery and detective stories.] I. Title.
  PZ7.S591857Fi 2005
  [Fic]—dc22

                                                    2004026075

Printed in the United States of America

for my mother
and
in memory of my father

1

So this is basically a story about a murder. It's a story about a murder and the fact that the cops said my dad did it. All implausible, but still a lot of trouble for my father. But I'll get to that. The story actually begins with a smaller crime. It was really just a way for me to earn a little money. And when I tell you what I was doing, you probably won't even think it was that wrong. Not really a crime. I was actually only stealing from myself, if you really think about it, although there are probably a few people who would disagree with me on this.

To set the scene, let me offer a preliminary description of myself. I was a poor kid trapped in the surroundings of great wealth and opulence. To be specific, I had a super-rich father who gave me nothing, afraid that if he handed over too much, I'd become the kind of spoiled-brat kid that he spent his life hating—he, by the way, did not begin life with any money at all. Now, I hate spoiled brats as much as the next guy. Show me a spoiled brat, and I'll hate him. But I believe in a kind of middle road, a kind of evenhandedness about things. I mean, maybe I didn't have to have the things of a wealthy man. Maybe I could live without a new Porsche or Ferrari, even though it was in my father's power to give me such things. But my dad refused me access to anything with a motor, including his car. Nothing. I got nothing. Nothing fun, at any rate. For instance, on my sixteenth birthday, the day I got my license, my father got me one of many savings bonds, to be cashed only when I reached the ripe old age of thirty-two. As for driving—out of the question. I even had to get my license using a friend's car.

And my dad also gave me a kiss. On my birthday. Once a year, on my birthday, he did this. He took me in his arms, hugged me, and kissed me on the cheek. A birthday tradition, although I know for a fact that he hated it as much as I did. But my father was a man of duty. His father kissed him every birthday. And that's the way it was going to be with me.

My dad was raised in northern Minnesota. His father worked on a pier in Duluth, which is actually a port town, even though it's locked in the middle of the country. But it's on a lake—a big lake, Lake Superior—and there are actually lots of commercial boats floating around up there.

Anyway, dad's father was Scottish and as much of a tightwad as you can find. He was also a Lutheran, which means that you and everyone you know are going to hell. It's an entire religion based on punishment. I'd even think it was kind of funny if this supposed punishment didn't also affect me so much. Anyway, my father's father died when he was thirteen, and to give you my interpretation of things, Dad always seemed to be dealing with this, even fifty years later (my dad is very, very old, by the way). Dad worshiped his father. And I guess he took his loss hard. And because of this, he always seemed determined to live up to his expectations. I think he was also just trying to keep control of things. He was a workaholic and a control freak, and I think that when your dad dies at such a young age, one of the ways of dealing with it is to do whatever you can to keep the world in order—after all, you've just faced as much chaos and disorder as there is. Anyway, point is that my father came from frugal and angry Scottish forebears. People who believed in hell. And as for heaven, it existed, but there was no way in. Not even for the best of people. Important for you to know.

My dad went to medical school at the University of Minnesota, and he did all right for himself there. In fact, as he always reminded me, he graduated first in his class. Then he went to a bunch of fancy hospitals in New York and then in San Francisco to "hone his craft," as he often said. He was most interested in cancer and cancer-curing drugs. Anyway, the story is long and boring, but the bottom line is that at a certain point, Dad decided not to be a practicing doctor, but instead some-one who owned and ran a high-end medical company. It was tight at first. Lots of experiments. Lots of tests. But no products and no real money coming in. Then his company hit the jack-pot. Came up with a so-called wonder drug for liver cancer. And almost overnight, my dad became rich.

My dad also had a partner. A guy named Jim Richmond. He was born wealthy, and he helped my dad get started. He was also a doctor and specialized in rare diseases. He worked with vaccinations for some pretty grim things, like smallpox—a virus that can also be used as a pretty powerful biological weapon. Richmond did a lot of work for the U.S. government on this problem. Top secret stuff. Terrorist attacks, biological warfare, etc. High-security matters that sometimes involved him with pretty powerful, badass people. The company had what's known as a hot lab. That means they kept live smallpox strains at the company. Not many hot labs in the world, fortunately. Anyway, that's important for you to know. The smallpox and the government thing. You'll need to know that. A major part of my story.

Anyway, they started the company in Seattle (where I live now), and not long after that, my dad got married and had me. He was fifty-four (old!) when I came along. My mother was thirty-five and also a doctor. She died when I was eleven, and frankly, I don't really want to talk about it right now. I'll get to her later, I guess. For now what you need to know is that I was raised by my old lunatic Lutheran Scottish father, who believed that good child rearing involved complete poverty and a kiss on every birthday.

2

B ack to the small and slightly illegal operation I had going. I was always strapped for cash, so it was absolutely essential that I had this little racket. Here's how it worked. Rather than give me an allowance, my father allowed me to work as an office slave at his company (which, by the way, was called Macalister-Richmond Industries, or MRI). The main offices were actually pretty big. About three hundred people (all extremely brainy) worked there. The main office complex—or "campus," as they called it—was also pretty big. They had a lot of money coming in and they owned their own building and about twenty acres of land surrounding it. The offices were plush. Really nice. And they were kind of cavernous. They overbuilt, as they say, thinking that they'd be expanding soon and that they needed to have space to move into. And they were right. The company was growing by leaps and bounds, as my dad liked to say. But there were still long, strange, empty hallways all over the building.

I worked in the marketing and sales department, where they basically figured out how to convince doctors and patients to buy their stuff. Now, you don't have to do much convincing to get a person with cancer to take your medication. But if you've come up with a kind of pain reliever or an allergy medication, you're dealing with a lot of competition, so you need a topflight sales force. Anyway, my dad liked me working in this department because it kept me away from the scientific stuff going on, which he was sure I'd ruin somehow.

"I don't want you near anything that you can break," he told me when I started.

So, as jobs go, it wasn't bad. But I got minimum wage—which just isn't enough for a man of my tastes—and most of the work was pretty dull. I photocopied things mostly. Sometimes I'd file things. I'd also staple things. And I'd remove staples from things. I'd also answer phones. Basically, I had all the jobs that an untrained, unmotivated high school kid can handle.

I have to say that I felt quite a bit of resentment about this job. My dad insisted that I go to the most boring, uptight private school there was, and having to slog away after school and on weekends to earn money for things as simple as sneakers and blue jeans seemed especially unfair. I mean, if my dad was broke, I could see the whole situation with a bit more maturity, maybe. If you don't have it, you can't really give it to your children. Fair enough. But given the fact that my dad was loaded, it was pretty rough, especially because he gave me *absolutely nothing*.

Anyway, here's what I'm getting at. Walk around an office building—especially one as crazy busy as MRI—and you'll notice that there aren't too many people watching you. Not many people keeping an eye on what you're doing. And I had the advantage of being the owner's son. People knew who I was and kind of avoided me, maybe thinking that they didn't want to get ratted on for one thing or another by the punk kid who was so close with Daddy. This, of course, was a joke. My dad would never have listened to me if I'd reported anyone. And if anyone was goofing off, I'd probably have joined in. And the truth is that no one ever really goofed off there—again, all really hardworking brainy types. But just because you're a hard worker doesn't mean you like having the boss's son watching what you do.

So here's the point: There was a lot of expensive stuff lying around and I was a teenage kid who knew the ins and outs of online auction sites. You can probably put it together from there. A high-end digital projector, CD burners, laptops, maybe even a printer or two. I'd walk them back to my cubicle—the humiliating place where they make you sit in an office—pop the items in a bag, and take them home to sell at auction online. Very simple, really. And a great way to earn extra cash. I was a very industrious young man. I think in lots of offices, they try to keep track of equipment. They definitely did at MRI. But they bought like a million printers a day there since it was growing so quickly, and it was impossible to keep on top of things. And the security measures they did have to prevent theft were pretty useless. Any reasonably sharp sixteen-year-old could easily bypass those. Now, my teachers and father might argue that I don't qualify as even reasonably sharp. But since I so successfully boosted equipment from Dad's company, I guess I'd have to say they're wrong.

I also stole quite a bit from Mr. Richmond (my dad's partner), who was kind of the entertainer and front man of my dad's company. He had all kinds of stuff that he bought with company money for the purposes of entertaining important clients and influencing the right doctors to come to work for us. You'd be amazed what a good cigar or a bottle of wine can go for these days. Hundreds of dollars sometimes. Sadly, you can't auction off wine or cigars online. These items are things the government really keeps an eye on. I mean, you can't have sixteen-year-olds ordering liquor and tobacco off the Internet. But I found a small and slightly crooked distributor in a kind of seedy part of Seattle—a liquor store and smoke shop called Albert's Indulgence that carried a few rare and vintage things. The guy there—Albert—bought whatever I brought him.

He was a little edgy about it at first. "Where the hell did you get all this stuff?" he asked when I first showed up with a box of cigars and two high-end bottles of wine.

"I stole it from my dad," I said. "And I can get more." This seemed logical to me. Seemed better than saying that I found it or that I stole it from another liquor store. Is it really stealing if you take it from your dad? Obviously Albert didn't think so.

"Well, I can't say I like the sound of that," he replied. "But I'm really just an ordinary guy trying to make a living here. So long as you're not really taking this stuff from anyone but your family and so long as you can keep your mouth shut, I'll sell it. But I don't know anything. As far as I'm concerned, you were just joking when you said that."

The next time I went back, I realized why Albert was so willing to take the loot. I got about twenty bucks for the wine and cigars. All together, he was reselling them for about $140. So, a nice profit for him. I brought this up with Albert on my second sale. "I think you're making a little too much money off me," I said.

Albert yawned, looked at his feet, then smiled and said that maybe we could work out a deal. He suggested that we split the take fifty-fifty, if I didn't ask for anything up front. "This stuff is hard for me to move," he said. "Most of my customers aren't the big-spending type."

I agreed to the deal and thus opened up another small stream of income for myself. It was unsteady, though. Richmond ordered wine and liquor and cigars like a maniac. But I couldn't walk away with too much, seeing as I really preferred not to get caught. A skilled thief always has to know when enough is enough. Getting too greedy is always the quickest way to get busted.

Anyway, the cigar and wine business was really just a sideline. Again, most of my cash came from office equipment. I should also point out that all this only goes to prove that I was some kind of young business genius. Amazing that no one ever thought of all this before me. But that's another story.

3

S o, let me begin to tell you about the murder that's at the heart of all this.

I first found out about it one afternoon after
school while on the way to a coffee shop called
The Standard. I was headed there with my two
best friends—Erika and Ruben. We were in Ruben's
car, listening to the radio, when the news came on.
The lead story was about this guy, Emil Belachek, who had
apparently been found strangled in his office. When I heard the
name, I kind of jerked forward in my seat because I knew him,
or at least who he was. He worked for my father, and as the
story continued, I found out that he had been killed at MRI.
The coroners were saying that it happened about a week earlier, though they couldn't pinpoint the exact time of death just
yet. Belachek's office had been locked over the weekend, and
for security reasons, the cleaning crew only ever entered when
the door was open. A custodian finally discovered him when
someone reported an odor coming from the office. According
to the newscaster, when they found the body, it was pretty
badly decomposed.

Completely shocking. Not something you'd expect at MRI.
And apparently the company was now swarming with cops,

although at this point, they still had no idea who had done it.

"We'll keep you informed of further developments as they come," the newscaster said.

The story ended just as we pulled into the parking lot at The Standard, although it was pretty hard for me to get my bearings at first.

"Unbelievable," I finally said as Ruben put the car in park and shut it off.

"*Really* unbelievable," Erika agreed. "Did you know the guy?"

"Kind of," I said. "I bet my father is losing his mind right now."

Erika and Ruben both laughed nervously. They had a pretty good sense of what kind of guy my father was, and the image of him dealing with all that mayhem wasn't a pleasant one. Really disturbing. But after sitting there for a second, we finally got out of the car and headed into the coffee shop.

So let me be up front about something—a tendency in my character. I kind of get distracted pretty easily. I'm kind of dreamy. It's a liability, but really something I've never been able to help. Anyway, hearing about the murder affected me. It did. And in the next few days, it was going to affect me far more than I could have possibly imagined. It was pretty much the beginning of the strangest time of my life. But as we headed into The Standard and looked around for a table, my mind began to drift to other things. Unfortunate, because if I had taken time to think about the whole thing, I might have saved myself some trouble. But it's just the way my mind works. And although the notion of the murder didn't entirely leave me, there was something else preoccupying me that day. Something that seemed pretty important at the time, although now I can't believe how dopey it is. There was a dance at Erika and Ruben's school in a few weeks—we went to different schools—and I wanted to know if Erika was taking someone.

We found a table, put our stuff down, I made a couple of comments about my miserable grades, and then, after a pause, said, "So are you going to your dance with anyone, Erika?"

"I don't think so," she said, looking up at the big menu that hung behind the coffeehouse counter.

Ruben quickly glanced over at me, kind of rolling his eyes— a look I got a lot from him—and then he stood up. "I know what I want," he said as he headed toward the counter.

So, for the record (and as may now be obvious), I was kind of nursing a major crush on Erika at this point. And it was starting to feel like a pretty big problem. I'd basically known her since I was six, and this (sadly) was the reason she said we could "never, ever go out." I'd never asked her out. I'd never even hinted at it. And I don't really think that she suspected anything. But the fact was that about a year earlier, I had developed an inordinate (some might say) attraction to her, and it had never gone away.

The reason it was a problem is that it just seemed like it

would never work. Again, as Erika often pointed out, "You're like a brother to me." She also said things like, "I could never like him. I mean, I could no more go out with him than I could go out with you." And, "I'm so happy we're so close—it's good to be friends with a guy who never tries to hit on you." And my favorite: "Evan, you're like a girl. You're such a girl. You're like one of my best girlfriends."

Not the kind of thing a man likes to hear.

Anyway, to be blunt about all this, Erika was something close to a Viking goddess. Nearly white hair, light blue eyes, a body that, frankly, you might find in a crass and reprehensible lingerie catalog (a thing I never look at), and a warm smile that let you know she was no snob. Everything you could want. And she was smart. Sharp as a tack. An amazing mind.

Despite Erika's profound intellect, however, she tended to go out with complete freaks. Tattooed bad-guy posers who a guy like me can spot as fakes from a mile away but who she always thought of as deep and artistic. She loved them all. And when they asked her out, she could hardly believe her luck. "Can you believe my good luck?" she'd say. "He asked me out! I can hardly believe it."

"Amazing," I'd always reply. "You really are a lucky person!"

I tried the jealousy treatment as well. Give her a taste of her own medicine, I thought. Sadly, however, this never seemed to work out. First of all, I could never really get too many women to go out with me. An astonishing fact. Second, the ones who would go out with me didn't last very long. Either they decided they hated me or vice versa. Well, maybe *hate* is too strong. But I've definitely had women tell me it was over in pretty bleak and cruel ways. And now that I think of it, there was never really any "vice versa." I was always the one being told to get lost. And that's no good if you're trying to make someone jealous. It's not like Erika would think, "Gosh, all those women keep dumping Evan. I think I might be in love with him." Really too bad that getting dumped isn't attractive to the opposite sex. I'd be living a much better life if it was.

So, kind of a tortured relationship. But this seems to be the only kind of relationship I ever have with anybody, so what was I going to do?

Anyway, back to The Standard. After a few minutes of inspecting the menu, Erika and I got up and ordered, and then the three of us spent the next couple of hours chatting, looking over homework, and getting jacked on caffeine before deciding to head home.

"We've got to go while I can still drive," Ruben finally said, shakily pointing to his eight-hundredth latte. This was smart thinking because he wasn't really the greatest driver to begin with.

Going home, though, wasn't such good news for me since I'd be dealing with a very stressed, angry, and (truthfully) very sad father, given what happened at MRI that day. Any one of these emotions always meant trouble with my father. He was a nightmare even when he was having a great day, so I wasn't looking forward to seeing him that evening.

Still, I had to go home. You always have to go home eventually. Sad, but true.

S o the ride home was quick but predictably troubling, and kind of descriptive of my life with Ruben.

Ruben dropped Erika off first, and as we pulled away from the house, he looked over at me and said, "You've got to let this Erika thing go, man."

"What are you talking about?" I replied. I deny everything, especially emotions—this is what I was always taught. It's the principal truth embraced by my forebears.

"It's never going to work," Ruben continued.

"What's never going to work?"

"This thing with Erika."

"I don't even know what you're talking about."

"I'm just saying you should take my advice and drop it."

"Drop what? You're out of your mind."

"It's time to move on."

"I don't know what you're talking about."

Anyway, I could keep describing this, but I think I've painted the picture adequately. Perhaps I should say a little more about Ruben, though.

I'd hate to call one of my best friends a total nerd, but

Ruben so completely embraced this identity that it would almost be cruel not to call him one. The fact is that he wasn't quite as weak and bookish as he pretended to be. It's true that he was a little scrawny. But he was just an inch shorter than me, had fairly healthy-looking wavy dark hair, and these friendly, warm brown eyes. With a few MTV stylists, he might even have been able to look as good as someone like, say, me. But Ruben would have none of that. He and Erika went to this open-minded and free-thinking private school called Holland-Cline, where they seemed to encourage people to be freaks and odd-balls. In fact, Ruben was sort of a king there—had the whole nerd thing going on to a T and was so talented at nerd things that everyone else thought of him as some kind of leader. I guess I shouldn't use the word *nerd*. I mean, I loved Ruben. Really. Few people in my life have meant as much to me as he has. But he called himself a nerd all the time. He'd beat me at a video game, explain some sort of complicated weather pattern, suggest some kind of new art project, etc., etc., and then say, "Dude, I am such a nerd." So, it was really a term of affection.

Ruben was also a major accomplice with my office equip-ment scam. Now, he didn't like this fact. Not one bit. But Ruben liked me, and theft from my father's company was sim-ply part of the package. Hang with me, you've got to help me with my crimes. A rule. Actually, Ruben always ended up help-ing me more than he wanted to. I'd explain some kind of angle I'd have, and Ruben (boy genius) would immediately tell me all the reasons why I was going to get caught. He'd say, "You're going to get busted and I'll tell you why." I'd then consider his reasons and act accordingly, heading off the problems that he pointed out. Ruben told me just how to adjust inventory manifests at the company, how to get rid of serial numbers, and even how to fake my identity with computer passwords. A real computer whiz.

But let me say again that I really loved this guy. For all the reasons you love a best friend. So I wasn't just hanging around to exploit his vast knowledge. I really liked him. And I have to say that as far as friends go, he was completely loyal and kindhearted. It was in his car that I got my license, it was he that took responsibility when I put a big dent in it, and it was Ruben that confessed to puking in my living room when it was, in fact, me.

I have to say that I also loved Ruben's parents. Extremely cool and relaxed. He could do absolutely whatever he wanted and they didn't care at all. They'd even fund whatever harebrained plan he'd come up with. Bought him all sorts of electronic equipment, computer stuff, and everything else a guy like Ruben would want. And believe it or not, Ruben stayed out of trouble for them. Sure, he'd help me with my various scams, but always against his better judgment. And anyway, staying out of trouble is a very different thing than not doing anything wrong. I, for instance, really didn't do that many things wrong. Sure, I engaged in organized criminal activity, but I was nice to

my neighbors, respectful of my fellow man, and only occasionally rude to my elders. So no real mean-spirited crimes. I, however, was always in trouble. Always. Could not stay out of
trouble at all. Ruben, by contrast, was just very good at keeping
his nose clean. Always knew when to leave before things got
out of control. And he was a nice guy. A really nice guy. So how
could any parent get pissed off with him?

The other thing that Ruben's parents gave him (and a very
important part of my story) was free rein over the large
detached garage they had—Ruben's parents were rich and had
a humungous mansion with all the trimmings. Anyway, this
garage had an apartment above it with a big open living room,
a kitchen, a bathroom, and all sorts of cool stuff like a pool
table, a dartboard, and video games. It was Ruben's greatest
asset—almost a reason by itself to become friends with him.
Best of all about the so-called garage, however, was that his
parents never, ever came in. "That's your space, son," I once
heard his broad-minded dad say. "So don't worry about your
mother and me intruding." So the garage served as our exclusive criminal headquarters and it was where we stashed the
booty I took from MRI.

Now, giving a kid so much freedom and so much unsupervised space may be a bit controversial. Not everyone would
think this was a good idea. But I'd like to argue that such liberal
and progressive parenting practices are in fact a model for all
parents of America, and I strongly suggest that everyone take a

lesson from these enlightened people. It is true that we ran a sort of criminal syndicate from the garage. That is true. But Ruben was sure to go to an Ivy League college. He'd probably get several advanced degrees. And he'd surely make millions of dollars when he finally got a job. It was his destiny. So, clearly so much freedom, so much access to resources, wouldn't prevent Ruben from becoming a smart, rich, accomplished member of our society. And what's more important than that? Ruben had highly liberal parents and he was going to be a whopping success. I (on the other hand, and to prove my point) had a prison warden for a father, and there was a good chance that I'd never amount to anything. You add it up. I think the conclusions are obvious.

Whatever. There you go. Ruben.

Anyway, the ride home didn't take very long—I lived pretty close to Erika—and in about five minutes, Ruben pulled up in front of my house. "So we're clear about this?" he said as we came to a stop.

"About what?"

"About Erika."

I opened the door and got out of the car. "Ruben, you really have to get over this," I said. Then I smiled, shut the door, and headed toward my house. Off to see my father.

5

The house was actually empty when I got home. Our housekeeper, Mrs. Andropolis, was off, and my father hadn't gotten in yet. I was actually thinking that I might be able to sneak off to my room before seeing him, but just as I was loading up a bowl of ice cream (the thinking man's dinner), I heard a key at the door, and in a few more seconds, my father's heavy stride was echoing through the back hall. He appeared in the kitchen with this look on his face like he didn't want to talk to me about anything and then just kept on going.

"I heard what happened today at MRI," I said, kind of weakly, and only catching sight of him out of the corner of my eye.

"I don't want to talk about it," he said, and in the next second, he was through the kitchen and headed up the back stairs.

That was easy, I thought. Then I heard him stop. "Have you done your Latin yet?" he called out.

"Yes," I said, which (needless to say) was a lie.

"You're lying to me, Evan. How many Fs am I going to see this semester?"

I thought about responding, but what was there to say? And

in the next instant, I heard him continue up to his bedroom, so obviously he wasn't waiting around for a response. A relief, really. And if I was quick enough with the ice cream, I could get to my room without having to see him again for the whole night, which, I decided, would be very fortunate.

Anyway, just to flesh this out a little bit, let me give you a few more details about this man I shared a house with.

My dad was mostly bald, except for a ring of white hair around the back and sides of his head. He had a white mustache that made him look like he was a big-game hunter—which he actually was. He had enormous feet. Astonishingly large, really. And he was also pretty tall, although his barrel chest and broad bald head gave him more of a stocky appearance. In the end—and this is more of a psychological impression that only a son can have—he was the kind of guy you would never want to see mad or yelling at you, which he almost always was and almost always did. Dad was a real yeller. An angry yeller.

For an old guy, I'd also say he was in pretty good shape. Did I already say he was seventy? Well, he was seventy. But being seventy these days isn't the same as it was thirty years ago. Strange, but true. Medical care is better, people know more things about exercise and nutrition, and there's generally just a different attitude about old people. Still, being that old did kind of make it like he was from another planet. His mind and body might have been in great shape—he was totally fit and as smart as they come—but there was the undeniable fact that he grew up in a very, very different time. When he was ten, for example, it was 1945. Think about that for a few minutes. World War II was still happening. Mind-blowing, in my opinion. I mean, his whole idea of childhood was formed over half a century ago. No one that old ought to be in charge of kids. Not joking about that, either. Maybe grandparents are okay, but they've already raised a set of kids, so they're working from a different angle. My dad was a total greenhorn when I arrived in his fifty-fourth year. And as far as I'm concerned, he totally blew it.

I don't know what else to say about him. He was fast. He was a fast kind of guy. I know this because he always chased me down when he got pissed off. Why he so often chased me down is a mystery. Maybe it's because when he started yelling, I tended to run. I tended to run while making brilliant but somewhat obnoxious remarks. But it's not like I really had anywhere to run to or like he ever tackled me when he caught up to me. Usually it was just a big fist grabbing hold of the back of my collar. Sometimes he'd take hold of my arm. He'd ask me just where I thought I was going or just what I thought I was up to, and I'd play dumb for as long as possible until he produced the broken vase, or the terrible report card, or the letter from the neighborhood watch association wondering why I wrote my name on the back of someone's house late one night. I will admit that I usually deserved whatever punishment I got. I am not a very responsible young man. Still, I could have done without all the yelling.

And Dad was a workaholic. Maybe that's obvious. But he worked all the time. This didn't mean, however, that he spent all his time at the office. He had a big study at home—with mahogany paneling and stuffed animal heads. The real thing. A real rich-guy joint. This is where he kept all his hunting stuff too, including bows and arrows, antique swords, and a big gun safe filled with guns. I was forbidden to so much as look at this safe, which, I have to admit, was probably good thinking on his part. No way am I the kind of guy who should be playing with guns. Even I know that. Still, the gun safe was always carefully locked, "just in case I got any ideas."

Finally, I should say that despite my general fear of my father, I was also quick to talk back to him. I don't know why. I've never had much ability to "keep my smart mouth shut," as he might say. It's true that it might have aggravated him more. It might have made him a bit more pissed off. But I knew my dad well enough to say that'd he'd be pissed at me whether I was talking back or not. Nothing I could do. So, in the end I don't think it really mattered one way or the other.

Anyway, there he is. We had a difficult relationship, to say the least. And (again) due to what had just happened at MRI, it was about to become much more of a problem. In fact, the very next day was when things slipped into something of a crisis.

6

So, the next day. Pencrest Academy. My school. This is where things started to get strange.

I was sitting in American history, trying to figure out what my teacher was talking about, when a student prefect appeared and said that I had to report to the headmaster's office immediately. Kind of surprising, and definitely not something that looked like good news. I went to a high-end, uptight, all-boys private school, where discipline was king and the tyrannical headmaster loved nothing more than to bully me around. My whole school, in fact, seemed to be designed to torture (or reform) a guy like me. Latin for an hour every day. French for another hour. Difficult math taught by angry Italian men. Half-hour lunches of brussels sprouts and diseased ham. Full-contact, violent rugby. And a bunch of students that seemed to love it all— thought that all that achievement and hard work was good for them. Little versions of my father. He was the guy who sent me there, after all. I think he hated paying the school's tuition—like I said, my dad was a total tightwad—but all that discipline and hardship was worth every penny in his eyes. Actually incredible that this kind of thing isn't illegal in our society.

Anyway, like I said, the prefect came, and in the next instant I was following him down the hall to the headmaster's office.

"What's this about?" I asked.

"Don't know," the guy replied. (Very unfriendly. The kind of muscle-bound, ultra-successful, top-notch student who hated "my type.")

So, puzzling. But I found out what this was all about soon enough. In another minute, I was sitting in front of the headmaster, who was silently staring at me, like he wasn't quite sure how to begin. Finally he spoke, and what he said was pretty unbelievable.

My dad, he told me with great calmness and sobriety, was in jail. He had been arrested that morning. For murder, apparently. Apparently, the headmaster said, he had stolen millions of dollars and murdered a man. "A man named Emil Belachek," he said.

I hate to say this, but it was just so impossible for me to get my mind around that I almost started laughing. When I think of murderers and thieves, I think of people controlled by unstoppable desire and passion. My dad was the most in-control person there was. Not a passionate bone in him. A bizarre obsession with my grades, maybe. But the idea of him killing Belachek was totally outrageous. I mean, just last night he was riding me about my Latin homework. "Are you sure this is *my* father we're talking about?" I finally managed to get out.

"Your father," he replied—the headmaster's name, by the way, was Mr. Perkins.

Again, I wanted to burst out laughing. I knew that this was serious—not really funny—but it was just so insane that I didn't know how to react. "I really think you must be mistaken," I finally said.

"No, it's definitely your father."

Pause.

"My father."

"Your father."

"Well," I said, still baffled, "what should I do?"

"Well, Evan," Mr. Perkins replied, "it's a very difficult problem. Obviously. But we all find ways to get through the hard times. In fact, it's just this sort of occasion that makes us stronger. You should think of this as an opportunity. In fact, you of all people should think of this as an opportunity."

Mr. Perkins leaned toward me as he said this, giving me a close-up look at his narrow, bald head—a head that seemed to bring his long, skinny body to a sort of perfect and harmonious resolution. Really. It was like an artist designed this guy. He paused for another moment and then said again, "An opportunity."

Another pause as I considered all this. "So what's next?" I said, still confused. "What should I do right now?"

"Well," he said, "I'll tell you what you need to do now. There's a man named Mr. Richmond—your father's business partner, as I understand it—who is coming by in a few moments to pick you up. I suggest you go out to the front steps and wait for him. I'll write you a pass, although you've missed quite a bit of school as it is. I'm not sure I'm very happy with all this."

"I'll certainly speak to my father," I replied. "I'll make sure he doesn't put us through this again."

Mr. Perkins glared at me. (I was pretty rattled by this point. What did he expect?) "Are you trying to be sarcastic, Mr. Macalister?" he asked calmly. "I suggest you begin to think about this in adult terms. I'm sure your father is innocent. I can't imagine otherwise. But it seems to me that this is not the kind of trouble you'd want to be making jokes about."

My headmaster wasn't a yelling man. He was, in fact, quiet, bookish, and not at all given to wild tirades. He was, however, a master of being disgusted. And his way of dealing with the more interesting characters of the school, of which he might say I was one, was simply to affect a sort of hopelessness—like, he'd bother to yell if he thought that it might actually help, but that, in fact, I was a hopeless and irredeemable case. At any rate, the headmaster wasn't really even the main disciplinarian. He was more like the academic boss. The discipline was left to a guy who had the unusual title of Pencrest steward. He was in charge of the screaming. I interacted with him quite a bit. He yelled at me all the time. Punished me ruthlessly. But I have to say that I think he also always kind of liked me.

Whatever. I'm getting sidetracked. For now let me just conclude by saying that I was told to sit on the front steps of the school and that Mr. Richmond was going to pick me up.

A fter about ten minutes, Mr. Richmond arrived. He waved to me from his car—a brand-new Porsche—and I quickly stood up and headed over to him. Mr. Richmond is actually kind of important for all this, so let me take a minute to give you a quick description.

Mr. Richmond wasn't like my father at all, which I guess is kind of strange since they were business partners. Mr. Richmond was relaxed, cool, and kind of acted a little young for his age—I'd say he was in his late fifties. He was always telling me to call him Jim, although my father absolutely refused to allow this. (Fine with me since I thought of him more as an adult than someone I'd call Jim.) Anyway, he was pretty tall and pretty athletic. He played tennis several times a week, ran every morning, and I'm pretty sure he went to a tanning salon, although I have no proof of this. He had sandy brown hair, dark brown eyes, and, frankly, a slick-looking smile.

I say his smile was slick, but the fact is that everything about Mr. Richmond was slick. Like I said, he was kind of the face of MRI, while my dad was the workhorse. That is, if there was an important visitor in town, Mr. Richmond would take him to swank restaurants to feed him lobster. My dad was more the kind of guy who sat walled up in his office all night reading medical journals. This is not to say Mr. Richmond wasn't smart. He was. He was almost as smart as my dad, which is saying something. Still, when the chips were down, Mr. Richmond was the businessman while my dad was the medical expert.

One other difference, along these lines, was the way they spent money. My dad had nice things—the best kinds of things you can buy, really. But they were simple, designed to last, and the fact is that once he got something, he didn't think too much about it. We had a huge house, fully furnished with British antiques and mahogany-paneled rooms. Nice, timeless pieces that would increase in value over the years. But things like high-definition TVs, swimming pools, and Porsches were strictly forbidden.

"We're not having any of that nonsense in this house," my dad liked to say.

Mr. Richmond, however, loved all that nonsense, and he couldn't buy expensive televisions and cars fast enough. He had a jet, too, but go into his office and there would always be brochures for bigger, more excellent jets—ones he just had to have. He also loved property. He had vacation houses everywhere. Hawaii, Jamaica, an apartment in London. Still, same with the jets and the cars, he was always talking about the next piece of real estate he was going to buy. Couldn't get enough.

Now, as crass and reprehensible as this sort of greed was, I have to say that there were plenty of times that I wished my dad was like Mr. Richmond. I, too, longed to look over brochures from car dealers, picking out the exact color I wanted and the exact kind of leather seats the car should have. These brochures, sadly, never came across my desk. I mean, it's true Mr. Richmond kind of freaked me out sometimes. As much as I was fascinated by the high-rolling playboy type—and as much as I wished my dad was that sort of guy—there was also something a little sketchy about the whole thing. I guess that's what having so many vacation houses does.

I should mention that my dad did in fact have a vacation house. Sort of. It was more of a tiny shack near Mount Rainier, not that far from Seattle. It wasn't the kind of vacation house where you sat by the pool sipping frozen cocktails. Instead it was the sort of place where you reclaimed your manhood. My father and I would go up there and spend the entire weekend chopping wood. Some fun. But my dad loved discipline and manly exercise, so that's what we did.

Anyway, you'll also need to know one other thing about Richmond's overblown self-image. Because he did, in fact, deal with high-level security issues like smallpox and bioterror, he was obsessed with protection. Had this freak thug of an assistant named Rick Colburn, who was always following him around looking tough. And along these lines (and believe it or not), Richmond often carried a gun. He had a license, which he obtained because he said he needed "extra security" given the sorts of things he dealt with. Frankly, kind of doubtful. In fact, it was kind of a joke. In my opinion, he carried a gun for the same reason he drove a Porsche—it made him look cool. Now, he didn't always carry a gun. But when he did, I'd often hear about it. He'd show it to me with a kind of hard-guy nonchalance, as though carrying this sort of thing was no big deal. It was also a poser, sissy gun. Long, silver, expensive, German. The kind of gun you'd see in a music video where some idiot musician was trying to convince you he was a tough guy. That said, the gun was real. There was no doubt about that. And I know that Richmond spent a lot of time at the practice range.

Anyway, I'm getting distracted. Mr. Richmond arrived and I ran down to the car. I kind of waved as I opened the door, but Mr. Richmond didn't even say hi. The first words out of his mouth were, "He didn't do it, big guy, so there's nothing to worry about."

"I figured," I said as I sat down. "But I don't even really know what's going on."

"You know Emil Belachek?" he said as he gunned the engine and sped into the street. "Our guy who got killed?"

"Kind of. I knew who he was."

"Well, the cops are saying your dad was the one who killed him. It's the most ridiculous thing I've ever heard. But that's why this is nothing to worry about. Your dad will be off the hook before you know it."

"Belachek was strangled, right?"

"Right."

"They're saying my dad strangled him?"

"It's pretty crazy, but that's what they're saying."

"Has anyone told you why they think he might want to do this?"

"Nope. I don't know any more of the story."

"What did Belachek do at MRI?"

"He was an ex-CIA guy. Worked mostly with NATO. Also with a lot of Eastern European countries. Everyone from Slovenia to Serbia. He helped governments set up plans to deal with potential biological terrorist attacks. And he did some security stuff for us too."

"Did my dad even know he was a suspect in all this?" I asked as Mr. Richmond roared through a light that had just turned yellow.

"I don't see how he could have," Mr. Richmond said. "Who'd have thought that? Your dad's as straightlaced as they come. No one in their right mind would have thought he'd be a suspect. But the police have narrowed down the time of the murder to last Friday night sometime, and apparently your father was on the premises at the time."

"But he's on the premises all the time," I said.

"I know," Mr Richmond said. "I know."

So, my dad was being held in Seattle's high-end federal building—the George G. Lewes Federal Building—and as we pulled up, there were a million guys in suits and sunglasses wandering in and out. The building had a jail in the basement, as I soon discovered.

After parking and walking to the building, Mr. Richmond and I presented ourselves at the front desk, where we were directed to an elevator.

"Take it to basement level 3," the guard said. "It's the last floor."

"Got it," Mr. Richmond said, smiling his happy but tough millionaire's smile.

As we took the elevator down and then got off on basement 3, nothing in the building really changed that much. That is, it really wasn't what I thought of when I thought of jail. (And I've been to jail before—more on that in a few minutes.) Everything was white, clean, and shiny, with bright lights everywhere. The whole thing looked like it was sprayed down with bleach every morning and smelled like it as well. It almost felt like a hospital.

"Pretty clean place," Mr. Richmond said, obviously thinking the same thing.

"Pretty freaky," I replied.

"It *is* pretty freaky," he said. Then he put his hand on my shoulder. "But let's not get worried here. Have to be tough for your dad. Everything's going to be just fine, kiddo."

There was another security guard right off the elevator who looked over a list when we told him my dad's name. He paused for a second and then sent us through another door behind him.

"Head down that hall," he said. "Tell the guards who you are."

In the next instant we were in another long white hall—again, kind of freaky. I almost wanted to see a rat or some lumbering, shirtless prisoner just to get out of that bright, sterile environment. But everyone was neatly dressed. Everything was perfectly clean. And as for any rodents living down there—out of the question. Nothing could live down there. No sun, nothing to eat, no water. Not even a cockroach could survive.

Anyway, when we got to the end of the hall, we met another guard, who walked us to a small room.

"You can sit down here," he said, pointing to a small table. "I'll bring Mr. Macalister in to you shortly."

As we sat down, I looked over at Mr. Richmond and flashed him a weak smile. I suddenly felt kind of bad that my dad was locked up down there. Mr. Richmond smiled back. "C'mon, buddy," he said. "Gotta be tough. This will all be over soon enough."

I was going to respond—was going to say that I was cool, even though this was kind of a lie—but suddenly the door opened and in walked my father.

8

Let me say this: No matter how crazy your dad is and no matter how much he tortures you by not buying you expensive stuff, you still kind of feel a sort of affection for him. Now, I'm not saying that this necessarily pertains to me, because the fact was that my dad was truly out of his mind—not just a little crazy—but as he sat down at the table, I've got to say I almost started bawling. My dad was kind of pale and looked pretty confused, and he was wearing this outrageous prison-style orange jumpsuit that I guess they put you in just in case you escape. And he had handcuffs on. Or they were like handcuffs, but there was a long chain separating the two bracelets, so he had a bit more movement.

There was some control in my dad's expression, though. He was trying not to let on that he was upset. He even spoke calmly as he sat down at the table. "Well, here I am," he said slowly. "I can't say I understand it. But here I am."

"You'll be out soon," Mr. Richmond said quickly. "I'll make sure of that. We'll put MRI's full resources behind this. They can't hold you for long, especially when they see what we'll be throwing up against them."

Mr. Richmond was a pro at being positive and putting his

best foot forward. He built an entire company around this talent. I, however, was almost speechless. All I could do was add a very weak, "Yeah we'll get you out of here." But when I said this, my dad just looked at me and rolled his eyes, as if to say that I was clearly in no position to help anybody.

"Well," my father finally said, "I suppose I'd be a lot more nervous if it weren't all so impossible. I mean, this is all so inexplicable that I'm sure it will sort itself out. It's just not a very pleasant thing to have to go through." Then there was a pause. "I have the feeling I'm not getting out anytime soon. My lawyer's already working on it. But I guess these guys are pretty upset."

My dad looked around the room. There were two guards and a big mirror—clearly a two-way mirror, probably with loads of agents sitting behind it.

My dad paused again, then said with a bit more anxiety than before, "What a calamity. Can't anyone see how ridiculous this is?"

Mr. Richmond grabbed hold of his arm. "We'll find a way out of this," he said.

I wanted to say something else. Again, I was kind of moved by the whole thing. Your dad can be a brute, but you still don't like seeing him chained up. But I have to admit that I was kind of at a loss. If this were a movie, I might have thrown my arms around the man and started weeping. But if I had done that, my dad would have cracked me over the head with his handcuffed hands. No ridiculous emotions or sentiments for him.

Still, I tried to think of something to say. But before I could open my mouth, my dad decided that he had a small point to make. He looked at me, his eyes kind of tightened, and then he lifted his hands and pointed at me.

"You," he said. "You. Mr. Cippiloni called me this morning just before they carted me off and told me you failed another math exam. When did you plan on telling me this? Did you think you could pull the wool over your old man's eyes? Don't think I can't keep an eye on you from in here. I've a good mind to pack you off to a military academy. I've got enough to think about without you throwing away your future. I mean, just how many math exams do you plan on failing this year? Are you going to be a junior in high school for the rest of your life? Well, go ahead, just so long as you know that come your eighteenth birthday, you're out on your ear."

For the record, let me just say that my dad's head could be on fire and he'd still be thinking of how I was throwing away my future.

Mr. Richmond looked a little nervous at this point. He knew my father pretty well, so it's not like he was surprised by this sort of outburst. But I think it still left him a little unsure of what to do. I think I looked a bit upset too—like my feelings were a bit hurt, which they were. Mr. Richmond kind of looked over at me with what seemed like pity—like he wanted to give me a hug. But I didn't break. I didn't look hurt for long. I merely said what I normally said in this sort of situation.

"Mr. Cippiloni just isn't a very good teacher," I said. "I mean, if he were, I wouldn't fail so many tests."

Now, I was well aware of how this kind of talk aggravated my dad. But I just couldn't resist. I mean, here we are visiting him in jail and he's screaming at me about a stupid algebra test. The only way out was to say something obnoxious. My dad just glared at me.

"My lawyer's phoning Mrs. Andropolis," he finally said. (Again, Mrs. Andropolis was our housekeeper.) "He's giving her explicit instructions about you. Don't think I'm not still in charge. And you can leave my car alone and everything else that you're not supposed to touch. I see all, Evan. I see all. So this"— he pointed around him at the clean, white walls and two-way mirrors)—"all this means nothing. Because I see all, Evan."

Anyway, again, meet my dad.

So, the visit lasted for about another ten minutes. Dad talked to Mr. Richmond a little more about legal things—things that my dad's lawyer was handling. A bail hearing had been scheduled, but not for a week.

"My lawyer doesn't seem to think they'll set bail, though," my father said. "Apparently some crackpot FBI agent believes I've stashed millions of dollars in a secret account. They think I'll flee the country if they let me out on bail."

My father paused and then repeated, "A secret account. I can't believe it. Of all things for me to have." As he said this, he kind of smiled, although it was a pained smile. It was just all so ridiculous, but the consequences of this farce weren't one bit funny. It really was some kind of joke, though. My father breaks no laws, especially financial ones.

My father also talked a bit about Belachek and the murder. He only knew bits and pieces since the story had come to him in a confusing way through his lawyer.

"Apparently, there are just a lot of things that don't add up," my father said. "An erratic travel pattern, missing possessions, blank spots in Europe where Belachek can't be accounted for, etc. The whole thing's a mystery to me. But he was murdered. That's a pretty good reason for the police to have a lot of questions. What I don't know is what the evidence against me is. That's what my lawyer is working on now."

"Well, they can't have much," Mr. Richmond said. "We'll get you out of here soon. I promise."

"The whole thing is just such a mess. Such a ridiculous, unexplainable mess."

Anyway, the visit wrapped up when one of the guards stepped forward and said, "That's time." Then he put his hand on my dad's shoulder and helped him to stand.

We all said awkward goodbyes—no tearful farewells between father and son. Just some grunting, another stern warning about "failing so many goddamned tests." And then we were on our way. The only really touching or sympathetic discussion I had was after Mr. Richmond and I left. Mr. Richmond seemed genuinely disturbed by what was happening. As we walked back out on the street, he turned to me and looked at me in a very troubled way, like he was trying to say something important. Finally he told me that he was just so sorry I had to go through all this. "I can't explain it, big guy," he said. "It's just so crazy."

"I'm fine," I said, and then added, "What a grouch, though. You'd think he'd lay off about the algebra for once."

Mr. Richmond smiled. "Evan," he said, "I want you to know that there's simply no way your father could have done these things. There's no way. We just have to wait for the cops to do their jobs and clear him."

I thought about suggesting that I thought it was entirely possible that my dad could kill someone. I wanted to point out, for instance, that my dad would kill me if he could get away with it. But since Mr. Richmond was being so earnest and sincere, I decided it was best just to say nothing. Rare that I use such good judgment. Given half a chance, I'll usually say something completely inappropriate.

Anyway, let me come back to one final thing here. Something I thought about on the drive back to my house and still think about today. I'm loads of fun when I talk about my crazy Scottish dad from northern Minnesota who never gave me a cent and liked to yell about how useless I was. But there were heavier things at stake. There really were. Like, there were times that I really wondered if all his bluster was some kind of deranged act or if he really did feel a kind of profound disappointment in me. It's hard to feel like you've let someone down, even if what they expect is entirely ridiculous. Whatever. The point is that I'm a funny guy, and I can tell you a million funny stories about my dad yelling at me, but a lot of times it wasn't so funny. Made me feel pretty bad. Anyway, here's an instructive story:

When I was fifteen, I spent a few months hanging around some dudes who were pretty bad news. I'm not friends with them now. But I was—for a little while. Anyway, we were downtown, walking around, kind of looking for trouble, when we headed into a drugstore and began to shoplift some stuff. It seemed funny at the time, and we took all sorts of things that we didn't even really want: hair dye, cough drops, instant coffee. It was kind of exciting, kind of fun, until we stepped out the door and were all quickly apprehended by a guy who appeared to be seven feet tall and just as wide. We were paraded back into the store, the cops were called, and the store manager insisted we be prosecuted because he had had enough of "the stupid teenagers that run wild in Seattle."

Anyway, we were taken to jail, and our parents were called, and one by one they showed up, yelled quite a bit (the guys all actually had decent, law-abiding parents), and then they sprang their kids. I, on the other hand, had a different experience. There were six of us, all locked up in the holding cell, and after three sets of parents came, my father showed up. He was furious, as you can imagine, and he gave me a long speech about how this was, in fact, the sort of behavior he had come to expect from me.

A fairly typical comment. But what came next was pretty surprising.

"And so, Evan," my father continued, "I've decided that you might really get something out of this experience if I let you spend a night in jail. So, I'll see you tomorrow afternoon. At one thirty. Right after I have my lunch."

And after saying that, he turned and left the little area right outside the holding cell. The other guys just looked at me like my life was worse than they could possibly imagine, and when their parents came to get them, they took their yelling with gratitude, knowing that at least they'd be sleeping in their own beds that night.

So that was pretty rough, and that day, and that night, and the following morning, all alone in the tiny cells they have in the police headquarters, I was pretty miserable. And I have to say that I didn't even get it that bad. The cops were all super-nice to me. They put me in my own cell. They brought me extra food. And they even gave me a stack of Sports Illustrateds to pass the time. And all the while, they referred to me as "that poor kid" and "that kid whose dad is making him spend the night in jail."

Still, despite the fact that I had sympathy and a few magazines to read, it was really pretty terrible. Being locked up sucks. But material situation aside, the worst thing about it all was the fact that my dad had pulled this kind of thing. I mean, he was just such a mean bastard. And I really had doubts about what he thought of me. I mean, maybe he cared about me, but you can still care for someone and think they're a total loser at the same time. Strange, but what I really wanted was a dad who would come down to the police station, yell his head off, and then take me home to talk about what happened, to come up with a new plan for how I'd act in the future, etc. All the other guys had that. But not me. My dad left me alone in jail for the night. I mean, what does that say about my father that he'd let me suffer like that? What does that say about how he really felt about me? Hard questions, and questions that I don't think I ever really got over.

So, using this interesting and salient example, I have to say that driving home with Mr. Richmond, I did spend some time puzzling over the meaning of all this. In fact—and I hate to say this because my dad was in real trouble—I kind of enjoyed it a bit. It seemed kind of fitting. Don't get me wrong. I was also upset. I really was. But I took a strange kind of pleasure seeing my dad in a bit of trouble. The story he always gave me was that hard work, discipline, and diligence were the secrets to his success. And according to him, my lack of these qualities was the origin of my consistent failure. I mean, I suppose the guy had a point. But I have to say that I didn't mind my dad seeing that sometimes trouble comes your way when you don't deserve it at all.

9

So when I got home, cops were swarming around my house. I said goodbye to Mr. Richmond—he told me he had to get to a meeting but that he'd "check in on me soon"—and then I headed in.

When I first went through my front door, I actually thought I'd have to go to a hotel because things were so crazy. But the cops and FBI agents didn't take as long as you'd think they would. They'd been at it all day by the time I got home, so they only stuck around for another hour or so. I was given strict instructions not to remove anything that "might be considered evidence," although I wasn't really sure what this might be. And then they split. I do have to say that the one guy I talked to was smart and pretty nice. Agent Sam Diaz. He even said that he was really sorry about everything that was happening and that my father might well be innocent.

"There's just a lot of difficult questions we have," he said. "And this is just the way it works; this is just the way we try to find out what's going on. If we've got the wrong guy, we'll know soon enough."

"Well, my dad's a lunatic," I said. "But I'm pretty sure you've got the wrong guy."

Agent Diaz smiled and asked me if I needed anything. "I'm not sure I want you staying here all alone," he said. But just about this time our housekeeper, Mrs. Andropolis, showed up. She looked like she was going to have a heart attack. There must have been twenty people stomping through our house, all in uniforms and white gloves. I quickly told her that they were leaving and that everything was fine.

"I got a call from your father's lawyer," she said. "But who knew there'd be all these strange men walking through the house?"

"Yes," I replied, "who knew?"

Anyway, the cops left when they said they would but added that they'd probably be back a bunch more times. They also confiscated a bunch of stuff, like various files my dad kept at the house. As they left, Mrs. Andropolis looked extremely relieved. Then she turned to me and smiled and said that everything was going to be all right.

"I'm sure of it," she said.

"I hope so," I replied, not quite sure if I believed her.

Anyway, here's probably a good place to give a more detailed description of Mrs. Andropolis.

Aphrodite Andropolis was a kindhearted, spry, and some-what handsome sixty-five-year-old woman who, among her many distinctions, was the only person on the planet who stood up to my dad. Me, she was always nice to. I could do no wrong in her eyes. And if I did wrong, she'd always look the other way. My dad, however, could do no right, and whether it was what he ate or how he dressed, she'd always come up with something negative to say.

"Oh, no, you don't eat that," she'd say, "because no way you're going to die of a heart attack while I'm in charge." Or she'd say something like, "You look like a bum. No grown man I know would wear a necktie like that."

Always funny stuff. Really. But I had to be careful not to take too much pleasure in it all. Seriously. If my dad caught me laughing when Mrs. Andropolis scolded him, I'd be scrubbing toilets at work the next day.

Mrs. Andropolis had a little apartment in downtown Seattle, but she also had her own quarters in our house. Two rooms, to be exact, put in years ago when the house was built. They were actually called maid's quarters, but no way did we ever call Mrs. Andropolis a maid. We didn't really call her anything besides "Mrs. Andropolis," I guess, and I don't think there's really another way to describe her. When she wasn't around, my dad would sometimes refer to her as "that Greek woman," although never would he say this in front of her. Never. Would mean certain death. She was pretty proud of being Greek, though. Apparently there's a fairly large Greek population in Seattle. Don't ask me why, but it's true. I guess it makes as much sense as there being a large Scottish population in Duluth, Minnesota. Who knows why anyone lives anywhere?

Anyway, Mrs. Andropolis usually showed up between three

and five every day, about when I got home from school. Then she'd stay into the night, sleeping over about two nights a week. She stayed home during the day mostly because she had several soap operas that she watched religiously, and not even me violently puking because of the flu could tear her away from the prime afternoon television hours.

So, she showed up at five on the afternoon that I got back from the jail—it was a late day for her because she had been at the dentist. Mrs. Andropolis went to the dentist about once a month—she had terrible teeth that were always giving her trouble. She'd had some kind of work done that day, although it must have been minor because her voice was crisp and clear.

"Murder a man?" she kept saying as she walked around the kitchen doing various chores. "Murder a man? Him? Murder a man? Forget it. He's too stupid. He barely knows how to dress himself."

She also said, "He couldn't murder anyone. He's too ugly."

Especially funny, not just because she called my dad ugly, but because I found it so mystifying that she thought ugly people couldn't be murderers. But she was sixty-five, she watched soap operas obsessively, and she thought the world of me, so what could I say about it? I just agreed. "You're right," I said. "He *is* too ugly."

Anyway, the rest of that night was kind of weird. I just listened to music and played video games and wondered what was next. I did try to do a little algebra, but I was now a boy in a family that had serious, serious troubles. How could I be expected to concentrate? I actually found a sort of strange relief in my dad's problems. This did, in fact, provide me a pretty solid excuse that I might be able to use the next day: "I'm sorry I didn't do my homework, Mr. Cippiloni, but see, my dad is a murderer." Might work, although I never actually tried it out.

The next day I went to school as usual. Didn't pay attention, got back some less-than-average grades on quizzes and homework, and then returned home for the next round of briefings on my father's situation. I was actually supposed to see him again that afternoon, but apparently he was busy with the cops. Instead, I went home to Mrs. Andropolis, and I also discovered my dad's lawyer there. He was sitting in my dad's den and was on the phone with papers spread out everywhere in front of him. "Evan," he whispered, and pointed at the phone, "just give me a minute to wrap this up." (The lawyer's name was Mr. Ellis, by the way.) He rattled off some numbers into the phone—I don't know about what—then hung up, looked at me, smiled, and said, "Well, Evan, we're in a pretty big mess here. But it's also nothing to worry about. It will just take a little time for everything to unravel."

I just nodded, because what was I supposed to say? I actually liked Mr. Ellis. A nice guy, although also very businesslike. He also knew a lot about me since he handled so much of my dad's personal business. I guess he was the right guy to keep me updated on everything. Still, he didn't tell me that much. He just kept saying that my dad didn't do any of the things he was accused of and that he'd get to the bottom of everything as quickly as possible.

Strange, though. There must have been some reason the cops had to keep my dad. And this is what I said. "There's got to be some kind of explanation for why they've grabbed my dad."

Mr. Ellis kind of hemmed and hawed and said that the law was mysterious and that cops sometimes came to the wrong conclusions, but that he was sure they could work everything out. In other words, he was very vague.

Later that evening, however, I got a clearer picture of what was going on.

Ruben had come over and we decided to order a pizza. Now, ordering a pizza may sound like a simple thing, but Ruben and I rarely agreed on matters of food, so this actually took some time.

"I hate anchovies," I said, responding to his first (and somewhat hostile) suggestion regarding toppings.

"So get half without anchovies," Ruben replied.

"The juice always runs."

"What are you talking about? Anchovies don't have juice."

"They have oils. That's well known. Anchovies have oils. And the oils run. And I hate it. If there's one thing I hate, it's running anchovy oils."

Ruben glared at me. "Fine. Let's get two small pizzas. You can get what you want on yours. I'll get what I want on mine."

"No can do," I replied. "I hate the smell of anchovies. If I smell anchovies, I can't eat. It will ruin eating for me. And I'll tell you something else. Once anchovy smell starts floating around your house, it's almost impossible to get out. I'll have to sleep with anchovy smell everywhere. Can you imagine that?"

Again, Ruben glared at me. He was getting upset, apparently. "Is there any chance of me winning this one?" he finally asked. "I mean, is there a point in me continuing?" I have a unique talent for exhausting people. I developed this ability with my dad, but I can apply it to almost anybody. It's a great way to win an argument. But you've got to be careful not to take it too far.

"You can get anchovies if you eat your pizza in the bathroom," I said.

"I'm not eating in the bathroom."

"The basement, then."

"Not the basement either."

"Okay. Then you have to pay."

"I'd have to pay anyway. I always pay."

"Okay, then, it's settled: You pay. But can you please ask the pizza man to wipe the anchovies off before putting them on your pizza?"

Ruben was now kind of snarling, but he managed to keep it together enough to pick up the phone and dial in our order. Looking back, I do think it was a good thing that Ruben and I could still bicker about unimportant things in the face of such serious stuff going on in my life. In fact, I'd say it's proof positive that I'm a very cool man. If your dad's going down for murder and you can argue about pizza toppings, it means you're keeping your cool. My dad might say that this was another example of me getting my priorities mixed up. But what's more important than dinner? I can't live in a world where dinner isn't my top priority.

Anyway, the pizza came about the time the local news started. Ruben had actually come over for support, although I was obviously not acting very grateful. But I was. Once I was seated in front of the tube with a big Coke and a slice of pizza, it actually occurred to me that I was going to need him. I had seen a few promos on TV earlier that day. They promised a "full report on the Macalister case" during the evening news. And when the news actually started, it was pretty grim.

The press had already reported that my dad had been arrested the previous day. But tonight they were giving the in-depth story. That is, they were explaining some of the details that hadn't been released yet and that I certainly hadn't heard.

Here they are:

1. Apparently, my father had a secret bank account in the Bahamas—a place where bad guys often have secret bank accounts. There were ten million dollars in this account. And the cops suspected that there might be other accounts.

2. There was a kind of paper trail—virtual footprints, as it were—that led from my dad's company to the Bahamas account. That is, the money in the account came from Dad's company.

3. The FBI's theory was the following: My father was stealing money from the company—or from his partner, Mr. Richmond—and hiding it in secret locations. Belachek found out and tried to blackmail my father, and my father killed him to keep him quiet. Apparently, there were e-mails showing the blackmail. These e-mails would be released to the press shortly.

As the news was delivered, I could barely move. Ten million dollars hidden offshore in the Bahamas? Blackmail e-mails? Ridiculous. Really. Spend ten minutes with my father and you'd know he'd never do anything like this. But there was a dead man. And (apparently) my father had a fat and unexplained bank account. And people kill people over money. Happens all the time. So, it all seemed to add up in the FBI's eyes.

The press also said that my father was denying everything, that he knew nothing about the bank account, or Belachek blackmailing him, or anything else about anything that might be illegal. But if he was guilty, it wasn't very likely he'd be spilling the beans.

As the news story wrapped up, Ruben looked over at me and asked if I was okay. "This is pretty rough," he said. "I'm sorry I got the anchovies, Evan."

"Well, maybe he's guilty," I replied, trying to act tough. But I don't think it worked. I don't think I looked as disinterested as I wanted to. I think I was looking a bit freaked out again. And I know this because Ruben was looking freaked out as he watched me slowly stuff pizza into my mouth.

"I'm really sorry about this, Evan," he said. I was about to tell Ruben that I wasn't worried—that I was sure my dad would get off. But the news continued, and I wanted to hear the rest. They started talking about my dad's business and, more important, his money.

By almost any standard, my dad was loaded. A bona fide millionaire many times over. But as they said on the news, there are millionaires and there are millionaires. And as everyone must know, there are also billionaires. The news stories estimated my dad was worth about forty million bucks. I had never known any kind of an exact amount, so this was news to me, although it wasn't too far from what I'd suspected. Anyway, a huge amount of money.

But a strange thing about people with a lot of money is that lots of them tend to want more. And this is what they were saying on TV. As some idiot "expert" TV analyst said, "Evan Macalister wasn't satisfied with his millions, and greed seems to have driven him to the ultimate criminal act."

Pretty far-fetched. But that's the news for you. And again, there was a dead guy. And a big bank account. So there had to be some explanation.

Anyway, I suppose it wasn't too far from what I should have expected. I knew my dad had been arrested, after all. I had seen him in his orange jumpsuit. But it was all pretty rough to see it laid out like that. And as Ruben and I finished dinner, and then cleaned up, I was wondering what was next. I think I was acting a little skittish. Mrs. Andropolis was off that night, so Ruben offered to stay over—if I wanted.

I told Ruben that I was fine and that he should go home. "I know you're just itching to get back to your homework," I said as we stood together at the front door.

"Jokes aside," he said. "I really will stay over. If you need me to."

I smiled a little, trying to think up some kind of friendly insult to level at him. But as I looked up at Ruben, and saw his face, and watched the way he was looking at me, I was suddenly taken with this offer of friendship. It was pretty heartfelt. Pretty sincere. I almost didn't know what to say. Kind of heartbreaking, really. Finally I just said, "I'm not having your grades on my conscience. You're not going to blame me for missed homework."

Ruben kept looking at me with his big, serious eyes. He nodded and then said, "I'm serious, Evan. Whatever you need."

I just looked back at him, now more seriously, and said, "I know, Ruben. Thanks. I mean it. But I'll be fine."

Ruben hesitated and then said, "Okay."

And in the next minute, I opened the door and watched him head out to his car.

I walked around downstairs for a few minutes and then headed up to my room, thinking I ought to try to do at least a little homework myself. Still, I was pretty distracted. I was trying to get a handle on all this. The news had gotten worse that night. And I knew it was now probably going to get more confusing. I knew this. But I have to say, what came next was much worse than anything I expected.

The next morning there was a further development. The press was now framing the story slightly differently. Here's the headline on the newspaper that morning:

BIOTERROR!
MACALISTER TRAFFICKING LIVE STRAINS OF SMALLPOX

Stunning, frankly. Not good news at all.

S o let me tell you a bit about smallpox, since it was one of the big things my dad's company worked on and since it's now obviously pretty important.

As diseases go, smallpox is pretty much as bad as it gets. As you might guess from the name, smallpox gives its victims a pretty horrendous rash. It looks something like chicken pox but it's much, much worse. The pox cover the skin, and they almost always rupture and get infected. In fact, one of the ways that people die from smallpox is the total and massive skin infection that comes from the bursting pustules that cover the body.

Cells in other parts of the body are also damaged by the disease. Essentially, what you see on the outside—the pox—is going on on the inside as well. Lungs, the liver, the spleen can all be infected, with the virus ripping apart healthy cells, leaving them ruptured and dead.

It takes about twelve days for the virus to grow inside the victim's body before he even knows what's going on. This is called the incubation period. On day twelve, his temperature will shoot up—usually to between 102 and 106 degrees. That, in case you're wondering, is extremely high. Almost unsurvivable.

11

The person will also start puking like crazy and suffering from terrible head and muscle aches. About two days after the fever starts is when the rash appears.

If the case is extremely bad, the rupturing cells inside the body lead to massive organ damage and internal bleeding. A victim can also bleed from his mouth or his eyes or any other of the body's openings. The victim will also bleed beneath his skin, causing the skin to take on a dark, reddish color. Bleeding to death is also one of the ways people die when they have smallpox.

If a victim of smallpox does manage to survive—it happens—the infection (following the twelve days of incubation) usually lasts for about two weeks. After that, it's a toss-up how much damage has been done. A victim can be left with heart problems, liver damage, blindness, and of course terrible scars from the burst pox.

The disease spreads from person to person through the air, so if an infected person coughs, sneezes, or even just breathes, the people around him will probably catch it.

The other bad thing about smallpox is that there's no cure. There are vaccines, which help prevent people from getting the disease. But once someone has it, all doctors can do is put him to bed and hope for the best.

One of the reasons smallpox is such a threat as a bioterrorism weapon is that most people in the world—including younger people in the United States—aren't vaccinated. So if smallpox hit, it would absolutely devastate the world. Millions would die. Why are so many people not vaccinated? Well, the good thing about smallpox is that it was entirely eradicated in the 1960s and 1970s, at least as far as it occurs in the natural world. In fact, the last naturally occurring case was in 1977. So, this is not a disease that you can catch while you're waiting for a bus.

Still, live smallpox strains do exist. But they're kept under close guard at special hot labs—mostly in the United States. MRI, like I've already said, is one such place. These strains are kept around for scientific reasons but also because government officials are pretty paranoid that smallpox might one day be used as a weapon. And as weapons go, this one is pretty powerful. Want an example? In the first part of the sixteenth century, a Spanish dude named Hernán Cortés conquered the Aztec empire, which was in what is now Mexico. According to historians, one of Cortés's soldiers had smallpox during the conquest, and he introduced the disease to that area for the first time in history. What happened? The disease spread rapidly, and when the scourge came to an end, one third of the Aztec empire was wiped out—that's three million people dead. And many more were left permanently disabled and disfigured.

You can see why the U.S. government worries about small-pox being used as a weapon. If terrorists infected someone in the United States, millions and millions of people would die. And they'd die quick and terrible deaths. And it would spread uncontrollable panic—exactly the kind of thing terrorists are looking to do. The stock markets would crash, schools would close down, air and train travel would be suspended. Would be quite a catastrophe.

So this is where Belachek and Macalister-Richmond Industries came in. Again, they had what's known as a "hot lab," which basically means they had vials and vials of smallpox virus. They used it to prepare vaccines and to develop new sorts of vaccines—ones that might work better and faster—just in case strains of the smallpox virus ever fell into the wrong hands. Belachek was the company's liaison to NATO and individual European countries who wanted the same kind of protection the United States had. So say France bought vaccines from MRI, Belachek would be the guy who set up the deal and made sure it all went smoothly. Belachek was pretty much an expert on the subject and had worked for the U.S. government for years, looking at various forms of terrorism and bioterrorism in particular.

Anyway, in sum, smallpox is as bad as it gets. MRI had live strains of the virus. And the man handling the deals was strangled in MRI's corporate headquarters. Bad stuff. And now, the cops were saying my dad was tied up in it all.

12

S o, back to the story.
       I read the headline about the smallpox
thing that morning, but there wasn't much more
detail than that. Just that cops were talking about it.

That weekend, my dad was still hung up at the
jail. Still lots of questions, my dad's lawyer explained
when I called. Cops weren't letting anyone in to see
him—security had been tightened a lot. So I just hung around at
home and watched the news, most of which was taken up with
my dad's case. Obviously the smallpox thing was a big deal.
Apparently, according to the news, my crazy father, who really
had no pleasures in life further than bossing me around, was now
using Seattle as a base for selling weapons of mass destruction.

"Bioterrorism in Seattle!" the news announcer kept saying.

Next day was more of the same. Mrs. Andropolis came in
and watched some with me, and she had quite a few things to
say in response to the TV.

"Ridiculous, you stupid man!" she yelled when the
announcer started delivering the story. "Totally ridiculous. You're
an idiot. I hate you. I hate the news. Everything they show on
the news is ridiculous. Ridiculous. You stupid man."

I had been prepped by the headline that morning, so I

wasn't quite as shocked. Still, I agreed with Mrs. Andropolis. Always best to agree with her. And she was making a big leg of lamb for dinner that night. So I had to be nice. I actually started thinking that a big dinner was about the only thing that could make me feel better. But then the news story kind of continued, and I learned a few new details about the case. One in particular caught my eye. Kind of startled me. A bit of a shocker. Yep. Made my blood run cold, in fact. And not because of my father. Instead, because this fact in particular presented kind of a humungous problem for me.

A HUMUNGOUS PROBLEM.

I should have known. I should have thought about it. Maybe in some kind of subconscious way I did. But if I did, I repressed it. It was terrible, though. Terrible for me, at least. Here's the explanation:

The cops had traced a bunch of frantic e-mails from Belachek to my father. They were all very cryptic. Very mysterious. For example, *Major hot-lab emergency. Leak. Origins unknown.* Apparently, this was one of the more comprehensible ones. The rest sounded like, *Going to Rome. Will report by phone tomorrow.*

And then there was a somewhat shocking and very straight-forward one, the very day before Belachek was murdered. It said the following:

I know what you've been doing and where your bank account is in the Bahamas. I know you have more—ten times more, I think—although I haven't located where you've stashed that. But I'll be in Switzerland in a week. If you don't come up with 10 M, I'm turning you in.

So, not much mystery there. As I heard the television announcer read this one off, it seemed pretty clear that this was where the cops were getting their info on the blackmail from. They, in fact, had a blackmail note. Or a blackmail e-mail, to be more precise. And they found it on my dad's computer, apparently sent from one of Belachek's e-mail addresses.

"But there are still many unanswered questions," the announcer continued.

One of these questions was why Belachek got so straightforward in his final note but was so vague in his earlier ones. The cops were also wondering if they could find a direct link between my dad's accounts (or the ones Belachek claimed he had) and the possible leak of the smallpox virus. Was there an obvious money trail?

The cops were optimistic about answering these questions. They thought they could find the answers. They were interrogating my father carefully. He wasn't going to get out on bail— not someone who might be peddling deadly viruses. So they had some time. Still, he wasn't talking, apparently. He said he knew that Belachek was working on a leak of smallpox virus that might have been coming from MRI. But he wasn't being more helpful than that. But there were also other ways to find these things out. These were top investigators. These were the

FBI's finest. They could do a lot of detective work on their own, without the help of their prime suspect.

There was, however, one very important piece of the puzzle that was missing. A crucial piece. Completely central. A completely central piece. The piece that was going to ruin me: BELACHEK'S LAPTOP WAS MISSING.

This laptop was Belachek's primary computer. But no one could find it. They looked all over for it. A missing laptop. Missing right from Macalister-Richmond Industries. This laptop might break the case wide open. Laptops have lots of useful information. People write all sorts of things onto the hard drives of their laptops. The cops thought that if they had his laptop, everything might be cleared up—who Belachek was meeting with, where he thought the hot-lab leak was coming from, who might be buying strains of the smallpox virus. No doubt about it. The cops really thought that this laptop could provide a lot of crucial information. A laptop. All on a missing laptop.

Now, let's take a bit of a break.

A little breather.

Think about everything I've told you so far.

Let's think back to how I opened my story.

Now, let me tell you the tale of an unfortunate young man who boosted things from his father's business, thinking he was only stealing insignificant items that no one cared about but that occasionally, once, in fact, happened to be an item of vital importance. World importance.

A laptop, you see, was a prize heist in my criminal operation. I mean, a good laptop could get me well over a thousand bucks at auction. Well over a thousand bucks. So, when I saw one lying around, I usually took it. Almost always took it. Anyway, as I heard about the missing laptop, it occurred to me that I might be of some help to the police on this matter, that yes, in fact, I would probably bring a great deal to their investigation.

Let me take you back now to the evening of Belachek's murder (although I didn't really piece this all together until they started talking about the laptop on TV). As it turns out, I happened to be in the building that Friday evening (about six o'clock, I'd say), not far from Belachek's office.

I had no idea what was going down. No idea. I'm generally clueless. A dumb teenager, as I'm ready to tell any cop that ever wants to throw me in the slammer. What do I know? Nothing. Nada. Zip. I'm very, very stupid. But I was around that night, the night of the murder. And there was this laptop. Just sitting there. A beautiful laptop. Just sitting there. Not far from my father's office. It was in a conference room, just at the other end of the hall from my dad. This was, in fact, one of my favorite places to steal things from. Why? Because if someone ever did stop me and ask me what the hell I was doing there, I could say, "I'm looking for my dad," or, "I'm getting something for my dad," or any number of things that would shut them up, because who wants to interfere with the boss's son on a mission for his father? Anyway, there was this laptop. The golden plum of my criminal enterprise. The ideal online auction item. So I took it. Why wouldn't I? Makes perfect sense. I would have been stupid not to take it. A real idiot. Think about it.

Now, it wasn't hard to figure out who the laptop belonged to. Not for a criminal mastermind like me. Found out right away. But what did I know? Didn't find out about the murder till a week later, by which point, frankly, I had kind of forgotten about the laptop. And I didn't know that the laptop would go on to be such a key piece of evidence. Really. Again, in many ways I am not a smart man.

Anyway, the point is this: According to media reports, the cops were desperately looking for Belachek's laptop. The laptop probably contained vital information. And I had this laptop.

As this fact dawned on me while I sat there watching TV with Mrs. Andropolis, the hair on the back of my head stood on end. I'm not being poetic there. It really did. On end. Mrs. Andropolis kept saying things like, "I don't believe a word of this. How stupid these people are." I just sat there thinking that I was totally dead.

But I didn't sit there for long. In the next minute, I was off the couch and on the phone.

"Ruben," I said after he answered. "I've got to come over."

"I'm busy," he said.

"Meet me in the garage."

"I'm busy."

"I'm going to run, so I'll be there in ten minutes."

"I'm busy."

I hung up, told Mrs. Andropolis I had to go out, and in the next second I was out the door and running to Ruben's, my mind racing with what I had just learned. *I've got to turn the laptop over,* I thought.

But there was a problem with this. The problem was that if I did turn over the laptop, I ran a serious risk of getting busted for my theft racket. (I'll give you the technical details of this in a bit, but my so-called electronic fingerprints were all over the laptop.) In fact, there wasn't a risk but, instead, an absolute dead certainty that I would get busted if I turned it over. It wasn't even possible to just leave it on the police station's doorstep.

I could also shut the hell up, I thought. I could drop the computer off a cliff. Set it on fire. Pretend that I knew nothing. Nothing. That's what everyone thought I knew. Ask my teachers, or the headmaster, or my father. They'd all say, "That boy knows nothing. Absolutely nothing. Thick as a plank."

However, as thoughts of eliminating the evidence turned over in my mind, I did think of something else: if in fact this laptop could be so useful to the cops, it could also probably get my dad off. I mean, he didn't do it. I was sure of that. So whatever was in this laptop might help him out. Thus, destroying the laptop might not be such a good idea. Of course, if I wanted my dad to get life in prison, it might. But even I, the tortured young child of a stingy brute of a dad, didn't think that was a good idea. I mean, I didn't really want him to stay locked up any longer than he had to be. After all, he was my dad. But he was just so mean.

What to do. What to do.

Still, I had a couple of other options—ones besides destroying the evidence or turning myself in. But I'll get to those in a bit—just trying to let you know what was going through my head. And along these lines, I need to say just one more thing at this point. Kept coming to mind as I was running to Ruben's and thinking about the night that I grabbed the laptop, the night Belachek was strangled. I saw some other stuff that night too, stuff that I really didn't understand till later but that's important for me to talk about now, which will fit in with the laptop.

It's strange, but when you've got a booming company, people stay at work all day and all night. You'd think all these rich guys would be off partying on their yachts. But they love work. Love it. So you can walk around MRI at midnight and you'll still bump into some loser lab guy who can't come up with a reason to go home.

Anyway, I saw some people that night. None of them seemed particularly like a murderer. Except one dude, who always looked like he had just iced someone. Rick Colburn— that guy who reported to Mr. Richmond—who had the title of security chief. Colburn had been a special-ops guy in the army and then worked for the CIA—like Belachek. But Colburn was a different kind of man. Never cracked a smile. Always wore a trench coat. And again, he was very tight with Richmond. Reported to Richmond exclusively, as far as I can tell, and didn't have much to do with my dad.

Anyway, this was the guy who was in charge of everything from security guards, to high-end surveillance equipment, to overseeing strategies for safely transporting vials of the smallpox virus. Whatever. This description I've just given isn't just to amuse you with my penetrating wit and insight. It's important. You'll need to know about this guy. For lots of reasons. But the most important reason is that I saw him walking swiftly down the hall just as I was swiping the laptop—the night Belachek was killed. Didn't think too much about it then, but I'll tell you up front that it wasn't a coincidence.

S o, Ruben's garage.

"You have what?" (Ruben was a bit surprised after I explained the situation.) "I don't understand. Tell me this again. You have what?"

13

"The laptop," I said. "Belachek's laptop. The one the cops are looking for. And technically, I don't have it. If you want to be very precise about things, you have it. It's here in your garage."

Ruben just stared at me for a few seconds. Bulging eyes. Clenched jaw. Tense throat muscles. He looked like he had just swallowed a razor blade. Very funny, really. Then he finally started talking again. "You idiot! I knew this was all a terrible idea. We're dead. We're dead. We're so dead. We're so totally dead."

It was in times like this that Ruben really showed himself to be the social misfit that he was. Was not cool and calm about anything.

"Please, Ruben," I replied. "You've got to relax. Everything's fine. There are any number of ways out of this." Obviously I wasn't really as calm as I was trying to act, but I felt that it was important to set a good example for Ruben.

"No, there's no way out of this," Ruben said. "And I'm dead.

I'm dead. I'm in this with you and I'm dead. I knew I should never have helped you with all this. In fact, I knew I should never have been friends with you. Right from the start I knew it. I knew I was making a huge mistake. I should never have started hanging out with you. I knew I'd regret it."

"Ruben, I really think you're making too much out of this."

Ruben again just stared at me for a few seconds. His face was kind of blank, except for the razor-blade thing. Finally he spoke again. This time more slowly and with more deliberateness.

"Dude, please tell me we didn't use the laptop. At least tell me that."

"I'm afraid I can't tell you that, Ruben. Had to check my e-mail. Had online games to play. Had songs to download. Really good songs that I wanted. Anyway, you're to blame too. You're the one who broke in. And it's such a sweet laptop."

Again, Ruben and the razor blade.

So, let me explain this a bit, explain why Ruben asked if I had used the laptop. See, lots of times I'd take a laptop or a printer out for a spin, just to see what was up with it. With a laptop, it was an especial pleasure because I was, in fact, looking through other people's stuff. It was like going through someone's closet when you're not supposed to. Pretty fun. Who says it isn't? And with Ruben, boy genius, at my side, there wasn't an encryption or electronic security system that could prevent my entry, especially when the laptop was right there. It's not like trying to bust into someone's Web site. You can fiddle around with a laptop all you want without anyone knowing. We did it for fun. Bad, I know. And if there's any doubt, let me say that it makes me sick to talk about now. But true.

Anyway, the thing with this kind of monkeying around is that you leave traces. You leave identity markers behind. So, if you were to get the laptop back, you could get another computer genius to find out just who had been using the computer, especially with me, because I'd do everything from send e-mails to download music. I left lots of traces. I entered lots of personal codes, used my DSL line, downloaded lots of cookies, sent lots of identifying messages, IM'ed people, you name it. Put my electronic fingerprints all over it. I even wrote part of a paper on this laptop. (One I got a D on, by the way.) And Ruben did the same. To use all his de-encryption software, for instance, he had to hook the laptop up to his computer, which leaves all kinds of traces as well.

This trace thing, usually, wasn't too much of a problem for us because before anything went to auction online, we always erased the hard drive. And we didn't just erase it; we did what's called a deep erase. That means the hard drive is completely wiped clean. See, normally when you erase something from a hard drive, you still leave traces—you don't actually erase every bit of data. Small bits of information remain, and even though they're small, they can get you in trouble if the right computer expert is looking at it. But Ruben knew how to do the so-called deep erase. So if he wanted to, he could wipe our tracks clean.

Completely clean. And frankly, this was important because we didn't want any potential buyer to be able to trace the computer back to where it came from because, obviously, we didn't want anyone to know that we had stolen it. The problem with the deep erase was that there were no half measures, no way to deep erase only part of the hard drive. It was all or nothing. Either that or take a year or two to walk through every bit of data—an impossibility. Anyway, this was all a bit of a hitch in this particular case, since completely erasing Belachek's hard drive meant erasing evidence that might get my dad sprung from prison and save the world from a smallpox outbreak.

I'm pretty much in the dark when it comes to most high-level computer problems, and all this is just what Ruben told me. But I will say that Ruben definitely had a million examples of crooks getting busted because they left identification markers on computers. And these were good crooks—crooks who knew about computers; high-level hackers and virus writers, no less. The other thing is, we could be pretty sure that in this situation, a fleet of FBI computer experts would be working the hard drive over thoroughly. They'd find everything. And if we turned it over anonymously, the first thing they'd try to find out was who had the computer, thus exposing our criminal enterprise at MRI.

"Dude, we're dead. We're totally dead. We're totally so dead." (Again, this is Ruben.) And then, "We've got to come clean. We've got to confess. If we confess right now, we're just two dopey kids pulling a scam. If we wait, we're dead. Totally dead. I don't want to be dead. I want to go to college. I want to have a family, get a good job. I'm not sure if you're really aware of what goes on in prison, but the part with the orange jumpsuit and the mean cops is just the tip of the iceberg. The tip of the iceberg, Evan. A skinny guy like me. It would be all over. It would be all over, and it wouldn't be pretty."

"Ruben, you've really, really got to relax. We'll do something. We're not going to jail."

"Well, let me put it another way: We're sitting on evidence that might break open a case about bioterrorism. And we're sitting on evidence that might be useful to your father. Do I need to remind you of that? Don't you think he'd appreciate a little help here? And let me just say that I'm not getting involved in any little war you've decided to wage against him. We're not doing something just to piss him off. I like your dad. Sort of. And frankly, I don't think he's hard enough on you. Because *you* are totally insane, and you have a lot of bad ideas that you somehow talk me into. A lot of bad ideas. You are a bad man, Evan. A very bad man."

Hmmm. Ruben was quite excited, but he did have a point. Still, I was sure that we could handle it all in a way that didn't get us in trouble. How could we do this? Well, I came up with a pretty good idea—in my opinion. I simply suggested that we open up the computer, find out what Belachek knew, and then proceed from there. Maybe we could figure out who had killed Belachek on our own. Unlikely, if you consider my intellectual capacity—I'm more of a poet than a logician. But Ruben was smart. He could figure things out.

"No way," Ruben said after I proposed my scheme. "You've gotten me in enough trouble."

"Well, if we turn ourselves in, you're screwed for life."

"Not if we confess now. We'll just look like stupid kids."

"What do you think Harvard is going to say when they see the police file that will follow from all this? Co-conspirator in industrial theft, witness in a bioterror plot, miscreant computer hacker. Not Harvard material, if you ask me. Maybe they'd look beyond it. Maybe. But my sense is that there are eight thousand other computer geniuses with spotless records who will have applications in at Harvard as well. Why would they choose a risky applicant like you? You'd just be potential trouble. People don't like potential trouble. Especially Ivy League schools. Turn ourselves in and the dream is gone."

Ruben wanted to respond. He really looked like he had an argument against this. Really looked like he was going to unleash some kind of brilliant response. But after a short pause, all he could do was moan a bit and say, "Evan, what have you done to me?"

I felt bad for a moment there. I really did. I wasn't a good influence. Poor Ruben was helpless before my expert powers of persuasion, and it's true that he never would have participated in any kind of corporate theft if I hadn't talked him into it. But he was in a different situation from me for lots of reasons. For instance, one of the reasons he was for confessing everything was that he didn't have much to worry about at home. If he got busted, his liberal parents would blame themselves and probably organize a family vacation to Hawaii where they could talk things through. I, on the other hand, would have my skull caved in by a seventy-year-old Lutheran who hates teenagers, particularly his only son, who "is the worst of them all."

Ruben again looked at me with a pathetic and pleading look. But it was a look of resignation as well, like he knew that the best plan at the moment was the one I was proposing. Still, I needed to push it one more time, just to bring him around completely. "We'll just go through the computer and see what's there," I said. "Maybe this will be easier to handle than we think. Maybe we're worrying about nothing. But if we have to, we'll turn ourselves in. Or we'll take our chances. We'll leave it at their doorstep. Maybe there's a small chance they won't link us to the computer, although my sense is that they'll go through it with a fine-tooth comb. And people as smart as you will be doing it. But you've really got to relax. We're not in trouble yet."

Ruben again glared at me and then said (full of sarcastic bluster), "Yeah, you're probably right. I am making too much out of this." He paused, then sighed, then said with a kind of frown, "But what else are we going to do?"

So, it was decided. We were going to go through the computer. Still, had to wait. I had to get home because I was now starving, and I couldn't get my mind off Mrs. Andropolis's roast lamb, which is really more important than anything. And Ruben had to study for some kind of physics test or something. "I'd tell you to come back tonight," he said. "But I've got to get an A on this exam. As silly as it sounds at this point. It's no good having a clean police blotter and a B in physics. I'd almost prefer a conviction to a B."

Anyway, in the next second I was on my way home.

So, I was pretty tough on poor Ruben. But you have to be tough on people like him or you'll spend your whole life cowering from authority. And you'll spend your life broke. I mean, if I had listened to Ruben, I never would have stolen a thing. And then where would I be?

But I was, in fact, torn. I really was. I mostly do things out of greed, self-preservation, and sloth (that's an SAT word for laziness). That being said, I was really thinking of turning myself in—confessing what I had done, telling everyone about my scam, and letting the cards fall where they may. Seemed like it might be the right thing to do. But then I went to see my dad again (which, according to his lawyer, took quite a lot of negotiating with the cops), and after about two minutes with that guy, I realized that doing anything to help him—or to get my ass in further trouble—was out of the question. Seriously. He yelled at me for like twenty minutes straight. About everything. I admit that I had failed a Latin exam and that a neighbor might or might not have seen me drinking beer in the front yard (I have no idea), but it was like I was the one in jail for murder and bioterrorist mayhem.

"Dad, you're being really hard on me," I finally said. "I never do anything really bad. I mean, you're lucky you've got a kid like me. Maybe you'd like it better if I was out doing drugs or vandalizing schools. Maybe I should be more like Ricky Josephson and sell pot and steal cars." (Ricky Josephson was a neighborhood troublemaker and an example I often turned to.)

Still, my dad was rarely convinced by this kind of argument.

"How the hell do I know you're not already doing that kind of thing?" he said. "You've been heading in the druggie-vandal direction your whole damned life. Anyway, I'd settle for a drug addict who could get an A on an algebra test over the kind of headaches you cause me. I mean, just where does your brain come from? Your mother was smart as a whip. And I'm a goddamned genius. It doesn't make any sense."

Anyway, by now one might be beginning to believe that I'm exaggerating things. And to tell the absolute truth, exaggerating is a thing I'm prone to do. But I'm serious about this. My dad really was a psycho. And if he wasn't a psycho, he at least had ridiculously outdated parenting techniques. I'm pretty sure that was a major part of it. I mean, maybe he really hated me. It's possible. But I also think that he thought he was being a good father by yelling and screaming at me all the time. Like a little tough love might get a guy like me to study harder. Whatever. I was living proof that this parenting strategy didn't work. As a student, I was pretty much a failure. I really wasn't good at anything, when I think about it. I was just charming, funny, and a joy to be around. I had what might be called personality assets. Intangibles.

I will say that this kind of behavior was also a bit extreme for my father. I hate to admit it. I want you to know what a freak he was with me. But this was extreme. That said, I should also say that he softened a bit as time passed. The guards said that we could only have thirty minutes that day—it was only the second time I'd seen him—and even my dad gets tired after yelling me for too long, especially about my grades. Upsets him too much.

I was also eager to change the subject, seeing that the laptop put me in the middle of all this. Needed to ask a little bit more about the case. And frankly, I was genuinely concerned about my father, as much of a hard-ass as he was. Still, I was a little hesitant at first—didn't want to give my dad too much to yell at me for. But what else was I going to do?

"So what's going to happen to you, Dad?" I asked when his yelling kind of died down.

"What do you mean, what's going to happen to me?"

"With all this. There've been lots of news reports. It all seems impossible to believe that they think you've done any-thing like this. But, well, it also kind of seems like they really do believe it."

My dad looked at me with a very angry stare—although he didn't really look like he was angry with me at this particular moment. And then the look of anger passed. It passed and was replaced with a kind of sad and desperate look. And then his eyes got a little moist, and it looked like he might start crying.

Then he said (in a tone much softer than I was used to), "Evan, there's nothing for you to worry about. It's all a mistake. I'm sure you know that. I'm sure you know that I wouldn't do these things. But it's going to take some time to sort through all this."

"But where is all this stuff coming from—the bank accounts, the blackmail notes? I really can't believe any of it."

My father paused again. Then he breathed out heavily and said, "I think someone is framing me, Evan. There's a side to my business that's pretty high stakes. And I'm afraid I'm involved in a rather complex situation."

"Did you tell this to the police?"

My father rolled his eyes. "Of course I told this to the police," he said. "But they don't seem inclined to believe me. Every criminal in here tells the police he's been framed. They just smile and say they've heard it all before."

"Who do you think's framing you?"

My dad hesitated, then said, "I honestly don't know, Evan. It's hard to even imagine."

I was about to ask another question, but a guard walked in and said that time was up. My father looked at me, again with a bit of desperation, and said, "Don't worry about me. I'll figure this out. You just stay out of trouble. I'll talk to Mrs. Andropolis every day, so I'm still safely in charge."

Then I stood up, and the guard pointed his truncheon toward the visitors' door, and my father and I both left the room.

All very rough. Maybe my father's situation is the sort of thing that might fill an onlooker with pity. But again, let me say that this man was relentlessly hard on me, so I had to maintain my distance. Couldn't start feeling sorry for the old guy. Anyway, I was probably going to be the one to save him, so he was pretty lucky to have me around if you think about it. And as for me saving him, I was actually about to head off to do just that. Time to head to Ruben's garage to go through the computer. Had to see what Belachek had been up to.

15

So, like I've said, Ruben's garage was no ordinary garage. This was a luxury garage of the Seattle elite. If there was a television show that profiled garages of the rich and famous, this garage would have been lead garage on the first day of the show. If there was a worldwide competition for the most beautiful garage in the world, this one would have won the grand prize. I could probably come up with a few more examples, but I think you get my point. It was a great garage. Kitchen. Bedrooms. Everything. And again, it was entirely parent-free.

Anyway, Ruben had already cracked the first firewall in Belachek's computer back when I initially grabbed it. That's how I was able to use it. But within the computer, there were further security lines. Tough ones. And Ruben had to get to work again.

Still, when I first arrived at the garage, our plans were delayed slightly due to the presence of the lovely Erika. Since I had never thought that she was the type of person who'd date a thief, I always managed to keep my underworld activities from her. Sometimes it was hard. Like, the three of us would be out to dinner at a swank restaurant and I'd pick up the check. She'd look at me and say something like, "How are you going to pay for this?

You're always complaining your dad doesn't give you any money."

I usually just told her not to worry her pretty little head about it and that it was all taken care of. Actually, on balance, I'd say that women almost never like it when you use the phrase "your pretty little head" when referring to them. Not thought of as flattering. Still, I said it. Kind of made me feel like a big man.

Anyway, Erika had just stopped by the garage to say hi and was on her way to some kind of yoga lesson—a thing girls in her school do.

"Was rugby practice canceled?" I said when I saw her. A common joke because no one at their school plays any kind of contact sport.

"Nice one, Evan," she replied. I was trying to think up some other sarcastic remark when she smiled, put her hand over my mouth, and said, "That's enough from you. Be nice. You're not nice enough to me, Evan."

She, Ruben, and I always teased each other, so this was no big deal. Was fun, really. But that kind of physical contact was tough on me. Her putting her hand over my mouth kind of ignited certain urges in me. I wished I was more mature. I wished I wasn't always thinking about our possible romantic liaisons. I liked her. Really. She was one of my oldest, best friends. But I'm only a man. So what could I do?

I pulled her hand away and said, "You're the one who's not being nice." And then, suddenly, it occurred to me to tell Erika all about the laptop situation. Might excite her a bit. She did, after all, like bad boys. But I thought better of this. There's a big difference between bad boys and stupid boys, and at this moment, I was feeling like a stupid boy.

Anyway, without more flirting, she split—yoga mat in tow. As she left, I just kind of stared at the door, looking like an idiot, I guess.

"Hey, idiot," Ruben said. "Snap out of it. We've got work to do." Ruben and I were compatriots and staunch allies when it came to women. Brothers to the end. But he did get a little bit nervous when I was in crush mode with Erika. I think he liked the way things were and didn't want to see anything get messed up. And I think I felt the same way somehow. I liked how things were too. Maybe this was how Erika felt as well. It's difficult to say. Still, the crush was a hard, hard thing to shake.

Anyway, back to the laptop.

Basically, there were two things we were looking for—the things the cops said they were looking for when they talked about the laptop on the news.

1. Documents that Belachek might have been working on that might fit in with the case—Word documents, spread-sheets, etc., etc.
2. Correspondence and, most specifically, e-mails.

Like I said, Ruben had already broken through the first firewall. But we quickly discovered that Belachek had layers of passwords throughout the computer. Almost every folder and every file had some kind of protection, so Ruben had to perform some kind of secret computer operation before we could look at almost every single file.

I should say, though, as annoying as all the security was, it was kind of thrilling to watch Ruben in action. Now, as you may have surmised, I'm not very impressed by tricks of the mind. I'm more of a soulful man. More of a poet and a dreamer, not a data cruncher. So all that fiddling about with a computer just wasn't my thing, unless I was auctioning something online or downloading music. But I have to admit that it was something to watch Ruben at work. It really was. He was always totally focused, running algorithm after algorithm to break into a computer. Sometimes he'd get it right immediately. Other times, it would take him a day or so. But he could always do it. And it was really something.

Now, it's true that good hackers are a dime a dozen in Seattle. It's like the world capital of mischievous computer geniuses. Still, Ruben, I think, had a certain flair, a certain panache, that put him ahead of the rest. And I always told him this. I'd say things like, "Dude, you're a genius," or, "I've seen this kind of thing done before, but you really are the best."

I actually needed to say stuff like this because Ruben was, in fact, often resentful of joining in on my criminal activities when he really didn't need the money. But his ego was a soft touch. Threaten it and he'd work harder. Compliment it and he'd work harder too. Really very easy. Just like how he described his own manipulations: "It's really very easy," he'd say after breaking into a computer locked down by the most secure systems known to mankind. "You just have to be patient and know what you're doing."

He said the same thing as he started ripping through Belachek's computer. "Child's play," he said. "I can't believe this is the best security your dad can get."

Cocky. But he earned it. Ruben, in fact, would have made a great terrorist. Could have controlled the world if he wanted. His only flaws were his poor diet, his grossly inflated ego, and his tendency to listen to much dumber but still somehow interesting friends (me).

But aside from the codes, there was another level of trouble. The problem started to be less the passwords than the actual legwork. Lots of reading. I mean, once we started going through the hard drive, we realized that there were hundreds of files we needed to look through. All with eerie names like Smllpx7 and BioHzrd5.

"I hope your dad is a patient man," Ruben said. "This could take forever."

"Well, he is in jail," I replied. "So not much he can do to us. He just might have to spend a few extra days there, which, I know from the lessons he's taught me, can only build up a man's character. Besides, you can work as fast as any FBI agent."

Anyway, as tough as it looked, we did think we could get through the computer. We thought this. But it *would* be hard work. Very time consuming. I think what we were hoping for was a kind of silver bullet. A Word file where Belachek might write something like, *I expect to be killed tonight, and my murderer will be Mr. So-and-so.* This, sadly, was fairly unlikely. Not many murder victims leave such nice evidence. But the fact was that we really had no idea what we'd find, so hoping for a silver bullet seemed as good as hoping for anything. We were also quickly disappointed by the files that seemed like they'd lead to something. Smllpx7, for instance, was simply a document detailing an outbreak in 1957 that had some relevance—relevance for everyone but us. And BioHzrd5 was a boring discussion of toxic waste disposal that had been published in the journal *Science*.

For several hours, Ruben and I broke codes, opened files, and then found absolutely nothing. The one thing that did look promising was that we got onto Belachek's Web browser and found that he had clearly been using it to check an e-mail account (or accounts) with Hotmail. It was easy enough to find that out—just looked in the browser's history. But as for getting into the actual account, that was pretty much an impossibility. This was mostly my fault. See, when I checked my own Hotmail address, I erased the address that had been saved, and this, sadly, was permanently erased and couldn't be retrieved.

"Why do you do that?" Ruben screamed when he saw my name in the Hotmail address bar.

"What?" I replied.

"Why do you do this? This." (He was pointing at my address.) "Why do you do this? Why can't you check your e-mail from your own computer? Or mine? Why must you play around with every-thing all the time? What's your reason? Please. I want to know."

Clearly he was upset.

I simply told Ruben that, in fact, I had no reason. It was just something I did. Strange how often conversations with Ruben sounded like conversations with my father. Ruben even occa-sionally remarked about this himself. "I understand your dad more and more every day," he liked to tell me.

Anyway, without at least Belachek's Hotmail address, there was really no way to go about getting into his Hotmail account. Wasn't as simple as running one of the password-finding programs that Ruben had. Very troubling, really, since those e-mails would probably have been pretty informative. But what could we do?

We worked till about 3 a.m. that night before packing it in, and I went home feeling pretty depressed. We had turned up nothing, and it looked like we could have weeks of work ahead of us, with no real sense that we'd even find anything. I wasn't in bed till nearly three-thirty—had to eat a big piece of cake that Mrs. Andropolis had set out for me—and as I lay in bed, I almost couldn't bear the thought of another evening reading through boring useless stuff.

The next day, however, I was back at Ruben's. Back in the garage.

S o, next day. Wasn't as bad as I thought. It 16 was bad for a while. For a few hours. Boring. Very bad. And then something happened. Something big. It was something of a breakthrough. Although it wasn't at all the breakthrough that we expected.

Like I said, we had been at it for a few hours, and I was growing extremely bored. (Did I already say that I can't do anything for more than an hour without getting extremely bored? Ask my teachers.) Anyway, I was sitting on Ruben's couch, watching MTV and drinking my third Coke. Ruben was fiddling around with the computer. He wasn't reading files at this particular time but was instead looking for hidden files and folders that might be buried somewhere deep in the hard drive. He loves that kind of stuff, actually, and did it for some time. Then, just as a commercial for a new acne cream came on, he said, "Huh." And then again, "Huh."

"What?" I asked, not really thinking too much because Ruben tends to get excited over some fairly unimportant things.

Then he said, "This is actually pretty interesting. Someone else has broken into this computer. Someone that's not us, I mean."

So, let me preface the following description of what Ruben found with a brief set of important suppositions. If Belachek was murdered, and if someone went through all the trouble to frame my dad for it, there was probably lots of other diabolical stuff going on. Stands to reason. And if there was all this diabolical stuff going on, then it would make sense that there were other people trying to get hold of Belachek's stuff, like, for instance, this laptop. We can suppose, in fact, that we weren't the only ones who had tried to gain access to Belachek's computer. This is what you need to know, because what Ruben had discovered was that someone else had, in fact, been spying on Belachek. How did he know this?

"I think someone has installed a stroke recorder on this computer," he said.

"A what?"

"A stroke recorder. A keystroke recorder. Spyware. Someone besides us wanted to find out what Belachek was doing. They installed a stroke recorder."

Now, I had no idea what a stroke recorder was, but Ruben explained it to me. Actually very simple, really. Not that high tech at all. But very, very powerful. And easy to hide. Basically, it's impossible to record everything that a computer does. And when things are sent in code, like a password, it's almost impossible to know what the password is if you're monitoring it from an outside source. A stroke recorder lets you spy on someone's computer by allowing you to see exactly what a person has been typing—a stroke recorder basically records everything a person types onto the keyboard. So, rather than recording what's on the screen or storing data in code, it simply says something like, on May 7, at 3:31 p.m., a client typed:

> www.jcrew.com [enter]
> navy blue crewneck sweater [enter]
> xl [enter]

You don't know what's on the screen. There's nothing really that even says that the person is online. But you can deduce what the person was seeing. In this case, for instance, you'd be pretty safe in assuming that the user was on the J. Crew Web site ordering a navy blue crewneck sweater, size extra large.

The cool thing about the stroke recorder is that nothing is encrypted. So, let's say you typed a password like EVANMAC47. It would probably appear on the screen as *********. But on the stroke recorder it would appear exactly as you typed it— EVANMAC47. The stroke recorder simply records which keys you touched.

"I think this is really good news, Evan," Ruben said, now getting more excited. I'll admit, however, that it took me a little longer to appreciate the importance of all this.

"It's good news that there are other people running around

trying to find out what's on this laptop?" I finally replied, again somewhat confused.

"Well, that's not good news," Ruben said. "But it's good news that there's a stroke recorder."

And the fact was, he was right. This is why it was good news. If Ruben could break into the stroke-recording program (which he did in about ten minutes), we'd probably be able to find some of Belachek's e-mail addresses and passwords.

And this is exactly what we did. Ruben got into the program, and we printed out the records. Of course, the stroke recorder records every keystroke. In other words, it records a lot of garbage, including everything I typed when I used the computer (yet another reason we couldn't turn it over). But after a little time looking through everything, we found the following entries, typed several times:

> www.hotmail.com [enter]
> salk999 [enter]
> poxviridae [enter]

and then, after pages of apparently unimportant things, entries like this:

> www.hotmail.com [enter]
> galen999 [enter]
> adenoviridae [enter]

and then, entries like this:

> www.hotmail.com [enter]
> fleming999 [enter]
> hepadnaviridae [enter]

The other thing that I should point out is that the stroke recorder had a small dating mechanism that recorded when each entry was typed. So, looking at the dates, it seemed that since the stroke recorder had been installed, Belachek had changed his e-mail address every few weeks. Pretty much a sign that a guy is covering his tracks.

The dating mechanism also recorded the last time the stroke recorder had been checked (by the other people, we can assume). It was about two weeks before Belachek's death. Whatever. That will be important to know in a second.

Anyway, we quickly got on Hotmail and checked the addresses.

The first two addresses had been canceled. So no chance of getting hold of those e-mails. Lost in cyberspace forever.

But the last one, fleming999, was fully functional (Belachek probably died before he had the chance to change it), and I have to say it was pretty much a gold mine. A direct hit, as they say. There were only four e-mail messages in this account. But they were pretty incredible. Here they are:

Message 1

Virus located. Ring out of Paris. Selling smallpox.
Definitely from MRI.

Message 2

Colburn is in on it. Very dangerous. Knows you know.
Be very careful.

Message 3

You may be right about Richmond. May be in as well.
But no confirmation.

Message 4

Come to Paris. February 20. Noon. Café Saint-Beauvais.
A friendly place. I have proof about Colburn. will give to
you. Be careful.

Each message was signed by the same person: LUBCHENKO.

All pretty stunning. Ruben and I just sat there looking at each
other after we finished the fourth message. Sure, we had to figure
out what to do with the information. But in that instant, we weren't
thinking about what the next steps were. At least I wasn't. I was
mainly thinking about what the e-mails said about Mr. Richmond.

"I can't believe it," I said. "I can't believe Mr. Richmond
could be involved with this."

Ruben had met Mr. Richmond before, although only briefly. Still, he knew him enough to have an opinion. "Pretty impossible," he said. "I agree. But it's not as unlikely as your dad."

"Seems as unlikely to me," I said.

"The man loves fast cars, money, and private jets. As rich as your dad is, I'd say he has to be the least greedy person I've ever met."

"But this is my dad's business partner. They're friends. And he's a really cheesy guy. Generally, cheesy guys aren't also bioterrorists."

Ruben just kind of looked at me, not sure of what to say. And I didn't know what to say either. It really was a shock. And I didn't believe it. But I was in the same situation as the FBI. As unbelievable as everything was, Belachek had still been strangled at MRI. Someone had to have done it.

"I'm not surprised about the Colburn thing," I finally said. "That guy's a freak. He definitely could have done it. But Mr. Richmond just doesn't make sense to me." Then I paused for a moment. "But Colburn does work directly for Mr. Richmond," I continued. "It just seems totally impossible. Totally impossible. Anyway, I guess this Lubchenko guy isn't sure either. Still, even the possibility is hard for me to swallow."

Ruben didn't know what else to say. We just sat there looking at each other, completely shocked.

S o there was the puzzle of Mr. Richmond's involvement. Stunning. But we had more immediate questions in front of us.

"What the hell do we do now?" Ruben asked. This was the question.

There were at least five important facts that surrounded these e-mails. Here they are:

1. Belachek was killed on February 17. This means he never went to Paris to get the evidence the e-mails promised.

2. The stroke recorder had last been checked two weeks before Belachek's death—that's two days before Belachek opened this new and last e-mail account. That means that the bad guys hadn't read these e-mails.

3. We could assume that Colburn, and possibly Mr. Richmond, were pretty unsavory dudes. And since Colburn at least seemed to be on to Belachek, it wasn't unlikely that Colburn had also whacked him. Made sense to me. Colburn was a freaky guy, and again, I saw him at MRI on the night of the murder, the night I lifted the laptop.

4. There were bad guys out there (i.e., Colburn) who would probably love to know what we knew, or at least to have

their hands on the laptop. This is important. This is what was at stake. We had the thing that both the bad guys and the cops wanted. Not good.

5. There was someone named Lubchenko out there who could probably help us a great deal.

All pretty freaky. Anyway, we did some quick thinking that night and came up with something like a plan. We decided to e-mail Lubchenko.

"Don't you think he might be a little surprised to get an e-mail from a dead man?" Ruben asked.

It was a good question. But what else were we going to do? "I think we can explain ourselves," I said.

We took about an hour to compose the message, and we (wisely) decided against revealing that we were a couple of dopey kids who had stolen a laptop. Instead, we introduced ourselves as "friends of Belachek" and said that we'd be very interested in what he had to say about Colburn. We also indicated that an innocent man was probably going to go to jail forever if he didn't help us.

And there is the matter of bioterrorism, we added, hoping to hype up the urgency of all this.

Anyway, we weren't sure what to expect from our request. But what choice did we have? Had to say something. So we did. And then we waited.

We actually figured it might take a few days for

Lubchenko to get back to us—he'd probably have to think about the wisdom of responding. We could, after all, be bad guys ourselves.

"I wouldn't respond if I were him," Ruben said. "No way."

"Well, that's because you're a complete coward," I replied. "My sense is that Lubchenko is probably a bit braver than you."

"Why are you always so hostile? You're always so hostile."

"I'm trying to help you, Ruben. It's time you became a man."

"Well, you're the guy to help me with that. Just look at how successful you are."

Anyway, Ruben and I bickered like this for a while, and after some time passed, I decided that I needed to head home so I could get some sleep. All this thinking was very, very hard on me. Before taking off, though, I decided to check Belachek's e-mail account again. Why not? Maybe Lubchenko had already replied.

When I logged on, I did, in fact, get an answer. But it wasn't what we had hoped for. Our e-mail had been returned.

Undeliverable. Unknown Recipient, it said.

Lubchenko had closed the account.

So that was that.

Pretty demoralizing news.

"Not good," I said, looking at Ruben.

"We're screwed," he replied.

But it was late, and I really couldn't think about it anymore that night. "Let's talk about this later," I said. "When I'm more alert."

Ruben agreed that this was a good idea since he was tired as well, and in the next minute, I was out the door and walking home.

Despite my weariness, though, I kept thinking about the whole thing as I walked home. Still, I wasn't able come up with any significant insight. The only solution I arrived at as I walked through my front door was to scarf down several big bowls of Cap'n Crunch, which I could now keep in my house since my dad was locked up. A real pleasure.

18

Next morning, I woke up just as puzzled, and went to school trying to figure out what would be next. Seemed like the jig was up and that I'd soon be making a trip to FBI headquarters. All confusing and very troubling. And that afternoon, things got even worse. Kind of had a little incident at the house that freaked me out.

Erika was over, going on and on about the latest book she'd read. "It's about violence and American culture," she said. "You have to read it."

"It sounds interesting," I replied, trying to sound as serious as possible.

"It *is* interesting, Evan," she said. "I don't know why you always have to be such a grouch."

"I said it sounded interesting. What more do you want?"

"I want you to care about the rising crime rate in our country and where it comes from."

"Look, babe, when your dad is in jail for strangling someone, then come talk to me about the crime rate in America." (Rare that I ever had such a neat and tidy response for her, although it *was* a pretty cheap shot.)

She apparently thought it was cheap too. She punched me

in the ribs and said, "Ever call me babe again, and I'll teach you something about strangling."

"All right, all right, you're not a babe. You're a woman."

She punched me again.

"What?" I said. "What am I supposed to say?"

"You said 'woman' sarcastically."

"I did not."

"You did so," she said, hitting me again.

Anyway, I could keep describing this baffling interaction, but what's the point? Where this story is really going is that about ten minutes after Erika stopped hitting me, something extremely strange happened. We were doing our homework. I had my math book open and was pretending to be interested. Still, I couldn't get the Lubchenko thing off my mind. I was really thinking that I'd have to go to the cops and confess everything. Making me feel quite sick. And then the doorbell rang.

Mrs. Andropolis was around, and she answered it. I heard some talking in the hall, and then Mrs. Andropolis said, "He's watching television. With his young friend."

In the next instant, the door opened. I looked up, and in walked Colburn.

I almost started to vomit. But again, I managed to keep my cool. Bursting into tears and screaming is way uncool in front of ladies. But what the hell did he want, I wanted to ask, but I was so shocked that I couldn't say anything.

Colburn just kind of looked at me. Then he said, "Mr.

Richmond asked me to come by to see how you were doing. He has meetings today; otherwise he'd be here himself."

I didn't say anything. He just continued to stand there—by an antique writing desk we had. Then he said, "I trust things are well, then. You're keeping out of trouble."

"I guess," I said, now sitting up straighter.

He looked at Erika and said, "I'm Rick Colburn."

"Hi," she said. "I'm Erika." I have to say that Erika also looked a little freaked out, even though she didn't even know anything. Colburn had on a long gray coat, and his tie looked tight enough to choke him. Very intimidating. I half expected him to pull out a long pistol and blow my head off. But there was no gun. None that I saw, anyway.

"I know you must be worried, Evan," Colburn said, now with a bit more emotion. (Although I will say that the emotion seemed pretty forced to me.) "But it's best to stay calm at times like this. You don't want to do anything that might make things worse." Then he flashed me this very slimy smile—first time I'd ever seen him smile, in fact.

Again, I didn't know what to say. "Is there anything you need?" he asked, after the pause.

"I don't think so. Mrs. Andropolis is here. She's kind of taking care of me." I suddenly had a prolonged vision of Mrs. Andropolis trying to wrestle Colburn to the ground after he had started strangling me. True, she was tough. But she was sixty-five, and I finally estimated that if Colburn wanted to kill me,

Mrs. Andropolis wouldn't be much help. Still, I have to say that the idea of her latched onto his back, smashing him in the face with her tiny little fists, did offer some comfort.

Anyway, Colburn was still standing there, looking at me. Finally I said, "Would you like to sit down?" It was weird having him stand there just looking at me. He really was a psychopath.

"No. I can't stay," he said. "I just wanted to make sure everything was all right. I'll probably come by again—when Mr. Richmond can't make it. If you need anything in the meantime, call me." Then he pulled out his wallet and handed me his business card. He smiled again, said, "It was nice to meet you, Erika," then turned and walked back out the door.

Now, I will say that Colburn was always a strange dude. But I don't think I'd be over-reacting to say that this was definitely an alarming visit, especially given what I had read in Belachek's e-mails the night before. I guess I just didn't have much experience with ex-CIA types who get fingered for being part of international criminal circles. The only real criminal I knew was me, and I was probably the least dangerous person on the planet. Of course, the bigger question was the timing of it all. Was this visit just a coincidence? Did he suspect anything? Looking at it logically, it wasn't likely—there really wasn't any way he could he know what Ruben and I had discovered. On the other hand, the timing was pretty strange. All mind-boggling—so much so that I totally lost track of where I was.

"Evan," Erika said. "You look like you just saw a ghost. Are you all right?"

I looked over at her. Frankly, she looked pretty freaked out herself.

"I'm fine," I finally said, my voice now kind of scratchy. "He's just kind of a weird dude. Just kind of freaks me out."

"I guess," she said staring at me. "To tell you the truth, he kind of freaks me out too."

S o, here's a summary of the now fairly dire situation.

19

Belachek was in contact with someone named Lubchenko, and they had an appointment to meet in Paris. Belachek never kept it because he was murdered. Rick Colburn, a man I've already described, was probably involved in the murder and my dad's framing—Lubchenko had said explicitly that Colburn was "in on it" and "very dangerous." Mr. Richmond, too, might be involved. Stunning, but also unproven. What was definitely clear was that this Lubchenko probably had his hands on some kind of important information—something that might help spring my dad.

As for me, I was now fairly certain that I had evidence that lots of people would like to have. My dad and the cops for one, seeing that it might help to explain Belachek's murder. They'd probably be able to find Lubchenko, even without the working e-mail address. And there was a bad guy—likely Colburn—who probably would like such information destroyed. And said bad guy had just paid a visit to my house to tell me to "stay calm."

My dilemma was that I couldn't turn in the laptop because if I did, I'd be dead—that is, my dad would kill me and I'd go to jail. But I also couldn't destroy it, seeing that it now obviously provided a way out for my dad. I also couldn't do the anonymous drop-off thing because of the so-called electronic fingerprints that I had left—at least, this is what Ruben said. I thought about writing it all down on a piece of paper and slipping it to Agent Diaz anonymously. (Diaz was the guy I met at my house.) But it would hardly be treated like any real evidence. The validity of the info was confirmed by the fact that it came from Belachek's laptop. No laptop and the evidence didn't amount to very much.

Now, I'm a relaxed guy. Normally very cool. I'm known for my coolness. All around Seattle. But let me say at this point that my cool and chill attitude toward things had all but slipped away. I really needed to come up with a plan. No joke.

Sadly, there was only one idea I managed to come up with. It was the only immediate thing I thought of, the only thing I could think to do. The weekend was arriving, so I decided to throw a big fat party at my house. Great idea, huh? Always a good idea to have a party.

Escapism?

Evasion of responsibility?

Cowardice?

Yes to all of these things.

Now, it might sound kind of cruel and kind of ridiculous to throw a party when my dad was in jail and I was sitting on top secret, vitally important information. But here's the way I was thinking. (1) It was more than clear to me that my dad wasn't just innocent, but so incapable of the crimes he was accused of that I was sure he'd be out eventually. Pretty sure, at least. (2) Given the fact that the guy left *me* in jail that night—remember?—I didn't think I needed to be sweating this too much. Not too much. (3) I was probably never ever going to have another opportunity like this again, since my dad never let me out of his sight when he was a free man. (4) What else was I going to do? I wasn't really going to gain anything that weekend by not having a party. I wasn't in a position to do anything. The party made no difference one way or another. Think about it.

Okay, maybe it was a bad decision. But the truth is that I did need to blow off steam somehow. Really. I was exhausted with all the drama. I needed to get my mind off things. The whole scandal was very upsetting, and there's nothing like having a houseful of friends to get your mind off such a thing.

So, seemed pretty clear. A party was the only logical thing to do.

The only real issue I had to deal with was evading the supervision of Mrs. Andropolis. Actually, not that hard since she didn't spend the night every night. Usually she was there two nights a week. My dad's lawyer had asked if it might be possible for her to stay more. But Mrs. Andropolis had a daughter who worked five nights a week as a hotel manager, and she had to take care of her daughter's kids. It was true that we could have done something else. It was even suggested that another one of Mrs. Andropolis's daughters could come by for a few nights a week. But Mrs. Andropolis had no concerns about me being unsupervised.

"It's your father that needs to be watched," she said. "He's the one who can't take care of himself. Just look at him."

This was actually a common refrain on her part. She was always saying that my dad would die without her. "He thinks I'm here for you, but I'm here for him. That man would forget to feed himself if it weren't for me." (And that was the truth.) The point is that there was talk of having someone come to spend nights with me, but it was kind of forgotten, mostly because Mrs. Andropolis didn't care and because as things progressed, and my dad's case started looking more and more grim, the matter was dropped. Ultimately, I think that Mrs. Andropolis just announced that she would see to everything, although her version of seeing to everything was to leave me alone. What a woman.

I decided the party should be Friday night. Colburn had come by on Wednesday, so I needed the party as soon as possible. (It was now about a week since my dad had been arrested, if you're wondering.) And Mrs. Andropolis would definitely be gone that Friday night.

I was actually a bit uncertain about how to get things started. Obviously, I had never really done this kind of thing before. But it turns out that throwing a party is pretty easy. You just call one or two people, and before you know it, every kid in the state is at your front door. I really did only have to make a few calls. I called Ruben and Erika, of course, because I wanted kids from their school more than dudes from my own. But I did call a few friends from Pencrest—guys who were slackers like me—so I did have some kind of school loyalty about the whole thing. I was, however, quite surprised at the fact that just about every-one from Pencrest came, as well as their loser girlfriends and everyone else they knew.

Now, as you might suspect, there was quite a bit of drinking involved at this party. I didn't get the kegs. I don't know where they came from. I didn't even know they were there till the next morning. Promise. Really. Swear to God. But there was lots of drinking. Lots of drunk people. That's how I knew. If lots of people are drunk, you can be pretty sure there's been a lot of drinking.

People started showing up at seven. At seven, I should point out, I was napping after eating half a pizza. But what did my schedule matter? My dad was in jail and I was playing host. Everyone in the city knew where the action was that night.

"Evan!" the first guests yelled when I opened the door.

"Yes!" I replied. "Who are you?"

"We're friends of Scott Kipling," one of them said. "He told us to meet him here. You're having a party, right?"

I stood there staring at them for a moment, thinking about the following facts: (1) I hated Scott Kipling—a square-jawed rugby player who went to Pencrest; (2) I didn't know any of these people one bit; and (3) I hadn't had my shower, and I wasn't looking my best, and there were loads of girls standing there. Suddenly, I felt like my father. Wanted to say, "Get your freeloading asses out of here, you freaks." But as I was thinking of some kind of witty thing to say, everyone just started crowding in, and before I knew it, the whole house was filled with exactly the kind of kids my father spent his entire life keeping out.

So, I should point out at this juncture that it's a risky thing having a million people over and letting them run wild through your house. And for the record, let me say that I deeply regret everything I did. Everything. And I regret stealing things from MRI. Really. If any cops ever read this and decide to chase me down, I want to say that I'm very, very sorry for everything I've ever done. But disclaimers aside, things got kind of out of control pretty quickly, and I didn't end up having much fun. Now, if we'd been at someone else's house, I would have thought it was absolutely hilarious to, say, go through the parents' bedroom—riffling through their drawers, looking in their closets, crawling around under their bed, etc. But since it was my house, and my father's drawers, and my father's bed, and since the possible consequences for me were, for instance, death, it was very, very nerve-racking having other kids do that.

Surprisingly (I will also say for the record), as the night continued and more and more people started showing up, it was mostly guys from my school that were running wild. That's what happens when you're never allowed to do anything fun. The minute you have no adult supervision, you go crazy. Just look at me. But I will also say that people were pretty obedient once I caught them and told them not to do what they were doing. So, if I said, "Please don't pour beer in my father's shoes," they would smirk and apologize and move on to their next project.

Anyway, let me offer you a couple of vignettes to illustrate the evening's fun.

1. I had just told a bunch of guys to stay the hell out of the attic—why anyone would want to go into my attic is beyond me—when I turned a corner and was face-to-face with a Pencrest guy with a primed bow and arrow and two other Pencrest guys with long steel swords (all taken from my dad's study).

"What the hell are you doing with those?" I yelled.

"I see your dad's a weapon collector," the guy with the bow and arrow said (another rugby player, by the way—named Topher Smith).

"Yes, he is," I replied, "and I know where he keeps his guns, so put those back before I have to start to get serious about this."

Topher gave me this look like his feelings were hurt. Really. He looked surprised and sad. The arrow was still drawn back in the bow and he was looking like he felt bad. "Dude," he finally said. "We're just having fun. What's the point of having a party if we can't play with your dad's weapons?"

"Yeah," the two guys with swords said. Wrestlers. Guys I hated and who hated me even more.

I paused. Was there really a response to this? "Gee, you've

got a good point," I finally said. "I'm sorry." Then I stepped forward, grabbed hold of the arrow, and told Topher to give me the bow and that if he was looking for fun, he should go find someone to beat up.

"What about you?" he asked.

Pause. "I'm your goddamned host," I finally yelled. "You can't beat me up. Find another skinny kid. You can beat me up on Monday." Amazing the kind of bravery (and the kind of idiocy) you show when there are kids with weapons walking around your house.

Topher looked at me for a second and then said, "Deal!" Then he looked behind him, and said, "Boys, let's go."

Then they all handed me their weapons and headed down the hall. "See you Monday, dude," one of them said.

I decided then that Monday was definitely going to be a sick day for me.

2. The worst thing was when these Pencrest freaks started going through my stuff. I can kind of live with my dad's privacy being violated. But not mine. I had actually just gone upstairs to use the bathroom—there was a line a mile long downstairs—so it's not like I was checking up on things. But then I saw this idiot named Jonah Lanchester rifling through my closet, laughing with these other idiot guys he was friends with.

"What the hell are you doing?" I yelled, which, I will say, was fairly unwise of me, because these guys were big and mean and they definitely didn't like me very much.

"Cool it, Macalister," Lanchester said. "We're just going through your stuff."

"I know, but see, that's not something I want you to do. That thing that you're doing right now is not something I want. It's not cool."

"Dude, don't be a buzz kill," a guy named Wolf said.

"Yeah. What've you got hidden in here anyway?" (Lanchester again.)

"Nothing," I screamed with a kind of absurd battle-like shrillness. Watching people rummage through your stuff can make you pretty pissed off—and dangerously foolish. I didn't get too violent, though. Good for them. I just ran up to them, ripped my boxer shorts and bathrobe out of their hands, and told them to get the hell out. "Get the hell out, you freak idiots," I yelled.

Lanchester kind of stopped for a second and looked at me. A big, badass Pencrest guy. No joke. Very dangerous. And he looked kind of pissed. But he also looked kind of confused—like he wasn't really sure if a guy like me was supposed to talk to him like that. But it was late, and we were at a party, so he took it in stride. He simply punched my shoulder as hard as he could (which was about as hard as I can imagine being punched) and ran off with his buddies, I think downstairs, although who knows what they got up to next. I slowly shut my door and sat down to rub my shoulder. Really hurt. Really. But then I heard a crash downstairs—a lamp, I later found out—and in the next instant, I was off to take care of the next crisis.

Anyway, the real craziness only lasted for a couple of hours—when the crowd was at its peak. Apparently, there was another party going on, and once people had sown the seeds of mayhem at my place, they decided to continue their spree of destruction elsewhere. Good for me, I guess.

I'd say about 1 a.m., things really began to die down. There were still about a dozen people there, but they were mostly from Holland-Cline (again, Ruben and Erika's school), so there wasn't too much trouble. Most people were hanging in our formal living room, listening to my dad's stereo (which I was never allowed to touch), and eating leftover Greek food they'd found in my fridge.

I would have joined them—I did in fact wander in every so often to check out what was happening—but by that time I was sadly drifting back into reality and thinking about the laptop and Colburn and Lubchenko. I was dead, and the party didn't seem to be helping anymore.

Ruben had also obviously been thinking about these things as well, and we eventually found ourselves alone in my dad's study, sitting beneath my dad's stuffed antelope head and his humungous gun safe, talking about what we should do next.

It seemed like an insurmountable problem. We had key information in my dad's case. But we couldn't turn it in. And the one person who might be able to help us—Lubchenko—was unreachable at the e-mail address we had for him. The prospects of us saving ourselves were dismal. "As bad as it gets," as Ruben kept saying. I did, however, manage to come up with a small plan, ill-conceived though it was.

Now, I should restate at this point that I wasn't drunk. Perhaps I had drunk a few beers. Perhaps. But I will say that despite my relative sobriety, my idea might be one that would spring forth from a drunken man. I suggested we go to the café that Lubchenko described as "friendly" and see if we could find him. I will remind you, though, that this café—Café Saint-Beauvais—was in Paris.

Ruben reacted pretty calmly to my suggestion but only because he wasn't taking me seriously. He said, "Yeah, right. Wouldn't that be something."

"No, really," I said. "What do we have to lose?"

Ruben looked at me and smiled. "We're so, so dead," he said.

"I'm serious about Paris," I said. "We can afford it. We'll use our crime funds. And travel like that really isn't that hard—not these days, anyway. It really wouldn't be hard to swing at all. If nothing turns up, what have we lost? And maybe we'll learn something. If we can get in touch with Lubchenko, we can solve a lot of our problems."

Now Ruben was looking at me with a bit more care, unsure whether to laugh again or begin to mount resistance.

"Look," I continued, "if we don't do something, we're definitely dead. Maybe we can think of something else. I don't know. But if not (and it looks like we won't), we should go to

France. If we do go, at least we've got a shot at saving ourselves. The worst that will happen is that we'll get a trip to Paris out of it. A last hurrah before we surrender ourselves to the cops."

Now Ruben looked much more serious, and with careful deliberation he stared at me and said, "No way."

"Ruben, think about it for a second."

"No way. No way. No way. No way. No way are we going to Paris. No way. No way."

But I will say that as Ruben said this, he also started kind of smiling. Kind of. He kept saying, "No way." But he was still kind of smiling. Maybe he was drunk. I don't know. But I took it as a good sign. Still, he kept telling me no. "Forget it," he said. "It's just too crazy. I can't even imagine trying."

"Do you have a better solution?" I asked.

"Yeah. Let's turn ourselves in and take our punishments," he replied. "I mean, digging ourselves deeper into trouble doesn't seem like such a good idea. Anyway, the word *friendly* could mean anything. Just because this Lubchenko dude described the place as friendly doesn't mean they know how to find him."

Ruben had a point. But on the other hand, what did we really have to lose? And a trip to Paris would be a good time— maybe the last good time we'd ever have.

"It'll be fun," I said to Ruben. "Will be one of the best times of our lives."

"We'll die," Ruben said. "We'll go there and we'll die. And then we'd be dead. A strange man in Paris named Lubchenko could get hold of us and we could get our throats cut. I mean, this is how things go when I do stuff like this with you. It's a miracle I'm still breathing."

"You know, you've got to trust me more, Ruben. We'll be fine."

Ruben, as might be expected, just rolled his eyes and groaned a bit. But he was also still smiling. He knew it wasn't a good idea. He knew the possible complications and possible terrible outcomes. But he was still kind of smiling.

"So what do you say?" I asked.

"I say no," he replied.

"C'mon. It's a good idea."

"No."

"C'mon. Seriously. We should do it. I'm not joking here. We really should do it."

Ruben looked down at his feet for a moment and then looked back up at me. "I'll think about it," he finally said.

As far as I was concerned, that was a yes. Ruben is like a parent. "I'll think about it" is always a yes.

"I'll start making arrangements tomorrow," I said, quickly standing up and heading out of the study.

"I said I'll think about it," Ruben called after me. But I didn't respond.

There were, of course, a few logistical barriers to this Paris idea—ones that I'd have to take care of in the coming days. But it really is easier than you'd think to jet off to a foreign country.

Surprising, but true. Just a few little details I had to take care of. But I'll explain those in a second. Just let me wrap up my account of the party.

So, since my story involves a girl (and since the reason to have a party is to get with a girl), I just need to give you a small report of what went down with Erika.

Now, I had imagined that playing host would set me up nicely with Erika. We'd be dancing in the living room, I'd look like this hotshot rich guy throwing a wild party, and she'd suddenly take me by the hand, lead me away, and tell me that we were always meant to be together. "I should have done this a long time ago," she'd tell me as she pushed me up against my bedroom door and started kissing me.

Sadly, this is not how things progressed. The dancing happened, but not with me. It was another guy that she was dancing with, and when I stepped out of the living room and then returned a few minutes later, she had disappeared. Where to, I don't know. Didn't want to know. I've always made it a point to stay out of Erika's private life. Knowing too much is simply too painful. But I can't imagine that I'd like where she went very much. But I am a gentleman, so I will say nothing more about it. Still, it occurred to me at that moment that I was a very unhappy and lonely man.

As I was staring at the living room—Erika now departed—Ruben came up and put his hand on my shoulder. "Sorry, man," he said. "She just left." And then, after a pause, he said,

"If we do go to Paris—and I mean 'if'—we should invite her along."

"So you're in," I said.

"I said 'if.'"

"That means you're in."

Ruben paused and then said, "Okay. I'm in. But only to get us out of trouble. I'm not going to have fun."

"Got it," I said. "I'll make sure you don't have any fun."

"Great," he said.

S o, the party was a magical success, except for the fact that I didn't win the hand of the lovely Erika, or the hand of anyone, for that matter, lovely or not. Still, was lots of fun to goof around my house with lots of people. And I kind of felt like I had done my part to make the social world of Seattle's youth a bit better. That's important. Always do what you can to make the world a better place.

As for the brilliant idea we came up with about how to spring my father, I had a bit more hesitation. Was it really a good idea to go to Paris? My conclusion was that it was not. Nope. Definitely, definitely not. Still, I am a fount of bad ideas. And I've never had a bad idea that I didn't follow through on. So it was set. Time to head to Europe to find Lubchenko. After a little planning, of course.

The first thing we wanted to do was bring in Erika. I talked about the matter again with Ruben, and we decided that this was, in fact, a good idea. This was now an emergency, and we'd need all the help we could get. I also somehow convinced myself that if I was flying to foreign countries saving the world, it would be best if a woman witnessed it. Especially Erika. What's the point of being heroic if you're not getting full credit from the people that count? Anyway, we could use her, especially since her French was excellent. She had studied it for years at school. I mean, I had as well, but my straight Ds suggested that I might not really be able to communicate very well.

Anyway, after I had cleaned up some of the party mess, I called her up to brief her on the situation.

"Erika," I said when she answered, "I have something to tell you."

"Okay."

"I'm involved in a major criminal operation, and I need to tell you about it now, in case things get ugly."

"Uh-huh."

"I don't want to involve you anymore than I have to. But I need to go to Paris to find a man who goes by the name of Lubchenko, and I need your help. I need you to come with me."

"Sure, sounds great. Paris. Crime. All things I'm into."

"Of course, I'll cover the expenses. And I'll do my best to keep you out of trouble. But this is really important. And not just for me. And not just for Ruben. The fate of the whole planet could be in jeopardy. The three of us could be the only thing standing between life as we know it and a world catastrophe. Have you had a smallpox vaccination? If not, you should get one. Very important. Could save your life."

"Actually, I've never really felt the need to get a smallpox vaccination. Strange, really. When do we leave?"

"In a week. Tell your parents we're going to my cabin."

"I could just tell them I'm going to Paris to save the world. I'm sure they'd understand. How long do you think we'll be there?"

"Five or six days? Could be more. It's hard to say at this point."

Erika's somewhat doubtful and slightly sarcastic attitude changed once we all met up at Ruben's to talk over the situation. Ruben and I slowly presented evidence of our scam at MRI and the fact that we had stolen the laptop. It took a long time to sink in. Erika just kept saying things like, "C'mon, you guys," and, "This joke is getting boring." But as we continued with our explanation (complete with a presentation of the numerous disk drives and video projectors we had stashed in a closet in Ruben's garage), she started to realize that this wasn't a hoax. And, of course, Lubchenko's e-mails were pretty convincing. Eventually, Erika's skeptical, bored reaction slipped away. She became, in fact, completely furious and completely shocked.

"You guys are completely out of your goddamn minds," she said. "You've been stealing computers and now you're keeping evidence from the cops? You're total idiots. It's just so stupid. I can't believe it."

She was a bit upset.

"I mean, do you know how stupid you are?" she continued. "You guys are the stupidest people I've ever known."

And then she paused, put her hand to the side of her head, and then kind of started laughing. It was an exasperated kind of laugh. A nervous laugh. But it looked like her anger had dissipated and that now she was just shocked. Just like Ruben always acted when I was coaxing him into one of my plans. This was good. Erika was a smart, thoughtful person. Really. Always knew how to keep her nose clean. But she was a bit of a troublemaker as well—it's why, I think, she liked going out with all those tattooed guys, for instance. And it was this troublemaker side that I was trying to appeal to.

"You guys really are out of your minds," she continued. "I mean it. This has to be the stupidest thing I've ever seen. I mean, you guys are really, really stupid." Again, she was laughing as she said this. But nervously—as if she was going up the first hill of a roller coaster.

"I mean, you are really, really stupid," she said again.

"So are you in?" I finally asked.

"In for what?"

"In for Paris. We're going to Paris. Have to. Have to find Lubchenko."

Erika just looked at me and laughed some more. "You're such a complete and total idiot, Evan. I mean, how did I end up friends with someone like you?"

"This is exactly what I was asking," Ruben said.

"Are you in or are you out?" I said. "I have to know. Need to get tickets."

Erika paused for a second and then started kind of laughing again. Again, nervous laughter. "Are you really going to Paris?"

she asked, looking like she had suddenly discovered we were aliens.

"We have to. And it's going to be great. So are you coming or not?"

"Well," she said, "if you're really going—I mean, if this is all for real—then I suppose I'll come."

And then I started laughing because the only thing more stupid than a stupid scheme is for someone who's much smarter (and generally a better person) to get dragged into it too. That's stupid. But what young woman doesn't dream of going to Paris in the midst of international intrigue? It was irresistible.

So, she was in. And in the next few days, we started to plan.

So I was a hilarious guy, up to all sorts of fun high jinks. Throwing parties, flying to France, etc. But let me restate something at this point: I really was, in fact, pretty scared. Ruben and Erika brought out the cool side of me. The more nervous they got, the more I played the dude who was tough and relaxed. But let me say for the record that I was well aware of the stakes, and I was starting to sweat it. My ass was on the line in several different ways, as was my father's, and Ruben's, and now Erika's—pretty much the only people in the world I cared about. Still, what could I do? Had to move forward. The one thing I kept promising myself was that if the trip to Paris didn't turn up anything, then I'd go to the FBI with the laptop. Hated to do it, especially for my mean, angry father. But I knew I'd have to. Again, I may be something of a selfish man, but I still usually don't like to hurt people.

Fortunately, there were a bunch of details I had to work out. And there's nothing like working out details to keep your nervous mind occupied. The following are some logistical matters I dealt with:

CASH

One of the issues was cash, which actually didn't end up being a problem. First of all, I had lots of cash stashed away from my various crime sprees. I was, in fact, a rich man, in the eyes of some at least. Still, spending all my own money didn't seem right, especially since I was actually doing my father a big favor. Why should I foot the bill? Anyway, I had a solution to all this. When my dad was arrested, he was at home. I had already gone to school and he was getting ready to head to work when the cops came. The nice thing about all this was that his wallet was still on his dresser when they carted him off. So, I had his credit card. I had his ATM card, too, but no code. Needless to say, he never trusted me with that. But who needs an ATM when you've got credit? Also, since my dad was named Evan as well (I'm the third), I could use the card with impunity.

Now, I should say that using Dad's plastic would put me in a new kind of trouble. There was the slight hitch that my dad might not like to see things like plane tickets to Paris on his credit card bill. But I had a way around this. I decided that if he raised a stink, I'd simply suggest that it wasn't me and that it must have been part of the criminal operation that tried to frame him. Also, there was a chance that he'd never get out of jail, and then I'd really be off the hook. And then there was a third and even less likely possibility. That was that I'd capture the bad guys, and, after finding out what I had done for him, my dad would forgive me and promise to be nicer to me—not really an option I counted on.

Anyway, it was all a foolish and completely ill-conceived

plan. But these are the only plans I know how to come up with, and you've got to work with what you have. And the fact is that I'd always wanted to steal my dad's credit card and blow a lot of money. This was my big chance.

So, I had cash and a credit card.

TIMING

So, timing was a bit tricky, but only a bit. Ruben and Erika had spring break the following week, which was extremely convenient and fortunate, but I had no break at all, which was extremely inconvenient and unfortunate. Now, you might imagine that my spring break was either later or earlier, but the fact is that I went to a school that did not believe in spring breaks or any kind of break at all. I should actually correct that. We did get a long weekend in the spring—a sort of spring long weekend—but most kids used it to sign up for this thing our school offered called "Leadership Weekend," where they headed off to a city like Washington, D.C., or New York to learn things like trust and teamwork—things I believe to be entirely useless. But that long weekend was actually a month away. So, technically, I didn't have any time off. Still, I had been through a lot, so I decided I might be able to award myself a little vacation. A little break.

"You're just going to cut?" Erika yelled when I explained this plan.

"This is an emergency," I replied. "My dad's been accused

of murder. And if I have to miss school to save him, I'll do it."

"You're going to get us killed," she said. "I must be crazy."

It was harder for me to argue against this point. Of course, me cutting school would get me pretty busted. No way around that. And I could never, ever explain myself because I couldn't admit to anyone what exactly I was up to. But what else was I going to do? Would just have to take my lumps. I've faced worse.

PERMISSION

Now, Ruben and Erika have liberal, free-spirited parents. This is true. But they might not have been too thrilled if they knew their kids were jetting off to Europe to track down killers. Still, liberal parents are generally the easiest to fool, and Ruben and Erika simply said that they were going to accompany me for a week at my cabin in the mountains, where we could explore, get lots of healthy exercise, and just be with nature. They cemented this proposal by explaining that I'd been having a hard time recently, and they thought it was important to spend as much time as possible with me. Fortunately, because of my father's stingy habits and his belief in the simple life at our cabin, there were also no phones, and in the mountains there's no real cell reception. So, Ruben and Erika didn't have to worry about staying in contact. They could buy phone cards and call a couple of times from Paris, saying they were using the pay phone at the nearby general store. But they wouldn't have to do more than that. A rock-solid plan.

As for me, permission was both hard and easy. It was easy in relation to Mrs. Andropolis. The plan was just to tell her I was heading to the cabin. She'd cheer me on because she loved me and supported whatever I did. As for missing school, she wouldn't care. "Those people at your school are monsters," she'd always say when I did something like fail a test or get busted for cutting. She hated Pencrest almost as much as I did. She was like the last sane person on the planet. Really.

The harder part was my dad, although I didn't actually need his permission *per se* since he was in jail. But I would have to explain why I'd disappeared (didn't go to visit him or to school) for a week. I decided I'd just have Mrs. Andropolis get word to him that I'd gone to the cabin after I left. He'd be furious— missing a week of school was unforgivable. "Do you know what I pay those people?" he was bound to say to me. But I could deal with it. I could deal with that kind of fury. That kind of fury would be small compared to what would result from me going to the FBI with the stolen laptop. That, I could not deal with. Anyway, I was always in trouble with my father, so what difference did any of this make?

PASSPORTS

Because the government is always trying to keep track of you, you've got to get a passport before leaving the country.

This is how the law knows who's here and who's not. Important if you're the government and you're interested in pushing everyone around.

Happily, we all had passports already. I had gotten mine two years earlier when my dad shipped me off to a kind of boot-camp-style place in Mexico for a month. It was supposed to teach me about the great outdoors and surviving in the wild. Let me tell you about the wild: I don't need it. I'm much better at surviving in a place like Paris, where I can get a steak at any corner restaurant. In the Mexican desert, there are no steaks and certainly nothing that looks like a restaurant. But I'm getting ahead of myself. All I'm really telling you is that we had passports because of my trip to Mexico, which sucked, and because Erika and Ruben were always vacationing in places like Tahiti and Jamaica. That also sucks—or at least it makes me extremely jealous.

TICKETS AND HOTELS

If I was heading halfway around the world to save my dad, I was going first-class. It was about time that I started behaving like the spoiled son of a millionaire—a thing I had always dreamed of being. So I booked three first-class round-trip tickets on Air France—they had the only direct flight from Seattle to Paris—and I made sure we had access to the deluxe rich-guy airport lounge. Did it online, which is easier than you think, especially if you've boosted your dad's plastic.

"This is a terrible idea," Ruben said as I was plugging everything in. "Your dad's going to flip. Maybe we should just pay for it ourselves."

"Ruben," I replied, "this is the best idea I've ever had. You just leave everything to me."

As usual, Ruben just groaned and rolled his eyes.

Next was the hotel, which wasn't that hard either. It was just a matter of finding the best and most exclusive hotel in the city, which was the Ritz, and booking three rooms there. I wondered briefly if I could get away with two. It was, after all, quite possible that Erika and I would be sharing the same bed. But I decided that might not be such a good way of making a move on her. Kind of clumsy to say something like, "You're in bed with me, tootsie," although I have said many things that are almost this ridiculous.

Ruben was a bit cooler about the rooms, which we also booked online. One look at the Ritz Web site and he was hooked.

"I can't believe this place," he said. "Maybe this *will* be fun."

"I told you I knew what I was doing," I replied.

Ruben just sighed and shook his head.

ACCESSORIES

I knew that I might regret it, but since I had my dad's credit card, I bought myself a few little extras for the trip. Now, again, it was highly risky behavior using my dad's money for too many ridiculous things. Still, I was now hunting bad guys on foreign soil, so risk was like my middle name. I bought (among other things)

• a suitcase that a European gentleman might be proud to carry—$750;

• a pair of leather driving gloves befitting a cultured young American sportsman like myself—$250; and

• a long, white cashmere scarf in case it got cold—$440.

Actually, I hadn't even thought of the scarf when I first went out. It was the beginning of spring, after all. But the beautiful woman at the scarf display insisted that I buy it. "You look absolutely magnificent in that," she said. Actually, she was totally ignoring me until she saw how much I had spent on gloves. After that, she couldn't get enough of me.

"Is it cold in Paris this time of year?" I asked. "That happens to be where I'm off to."

"Freezing," she said. "You won't last a day without this scarf." This turned out to be an exaggeration. But I didn't hold it against her. She was right. I looked magnificent. No arguing with that.

I also bought a large leather footstool shaped like an elephant. At the luggage store. This set me back another four hundred dollars. What was its purpose? There was, in fact, none. Certainly wasn't going to bring it to Paris. But it kind of struck my fancy. Kind of liked the look of it. The problem was that they were out of stock. I only got to see the floor sample. So I told them to deliver it when it came in. That's what rich people do. They have things delivered. The other (and more reason-able) things I bought were a few books about Paris, including a tour guide called *Nightlife in the City of Light*. This book was particularly important. Can't tell you how useful it was. I needed to know where all the hot spots were. Great that they have such books in the world. We should have read more books like this at Pencrest, I think. But I'm getting away from my story here.

S o my dad and I never talked much. You've probably picked this up by now. Was really a kind of one-way-street sort of relationship. He'd bark orders, issue commands, and reveal his displeasure. I simply listened, although sometimes I'd argue or try to explain why he was entirely wrong.

Anyway, because of this, visiting Dad in jail was kind of strange because what the hell was the point of it? What was there for us to talk about? Still, when I visited my dad a few days after deciding to go to Paris, I was getting the sense that he needed to see me more than he probably would have liked to admit.

Of course, he didn't reveal this need in any kind of normal way. I will remind you that this visit was also following my party, and (as I expected) he got wind of it.

"Keep your stupid teenage friends out of my house," he said. "I mean out. I never want one of them to set foot in my house again. Not even Ruben, who I'm sure would be a much better boy if it weren't for your influence."

"It was only a few friends, Dad," I said. "We were watching a basketball game on TV."

"Don't give me that crap," he said, waving his hand in the air. "I know you. This is probably the best time you've ever had. Thrilled to have your old man locked up so you can traipse around, devil-may-care, doing whatever the hell you want."

Anyway, he yelled at me like this for about twenty minutes. Nonstop. Nothing but criticism. How I was going to drive him to an early grave. How I was a disgrace to our ancestors, etc., etc., etc. The usual thing I got from him. But then, after twenty minutes, the yelling took a very strange turn. He had just again accused me of trying to give him a heart attack when he suddenly stopped, paused for a few moments, and then, kind of bowing his head a little, said, "I just don't know what I'm going to do with you, Evan. I just don't know."

Then he looked down at the table that sat between us, kind of shaking his head. For a brief instant, he looked like he was going to start yelling again. He looked like he was going to yell. Like he always looked. But then he just sighed. And it was a deep sigh. A sad sigh. And then he paused again and then said, "Oh, what's the point of all this? I don't know why I even bother." And then, "What would your mother think if she saw me like this? I can't bear to think about it. I just don't understand how I got into this mess. I really can't understand it."

Let me tell you something about my father. He never talked about my mother. He did a little after she died—had to, because there were practical issues at stake. But as time went on, she became a more and more forbidden topic. He certainly never said anything like, "What would she think if she saw me like this?" So to hear him say it now was really surprising. And kind of frightening. When you're used to a guy yelling at you all the time, it's kind of scary to see him break a little.

And then I started to feel guilt. First, I felt surprise. Next, pity. And then I felt guilt. I had bought the tickets to Paris. We were leaving the next day. Everything was set. But as I saw my dad sitting there looking depressed and talking about my mother, I felt like the worst guy in the world for not just turning over the laptop and letting way more qualified people pursue all this. I mean, what kind of a bastard was I? It was one thing to steal computers from my dad's company. But letting him stay in this situation any longer than he had to was just so rotten of me. Rotten. Terrible. Unforgivable. I didn't know what to do. Not at all.

But after a few more sighs, my dad started to regain his composure. He looked up at me, squinted a bit, and then the old dad that I knew and loved came back again. "I mean never, ever, ever can you ever have anyone in my house again," he said. "Not your stupid friends, or those tramp girls you hang out with, or anyone else. When I get out of here, we're going to change how things have been around the house. I can see now that I've been much too easy on you. Much too easy. We're going to embark on a new regimen. A new plan. A new mode of behavior."

As he said this, all the guilt and pity just magically began to slip away. He really was mean—I wasn't making it up. Sure, maybe he had the right to be mad at me for throwing a party. But that stuff about my mother meant something to me. It meant something that he was talking to me like that. And then he goes and ruins it by starting to scream at me again. Whatever. The Paris plan was back on. Although I should say, in the interest of truth, that not really all the guilt and pity slipped away. I still felt it. I still felt bad. But as is obvious from my actions, I was able to control these feelings. I was able to keep my compassion in check. An important skill for an international crime buster.

Anyway, there was no good reason why I couldn't pull all this off and spring my dad without anyone finding out about my theft scheme. No reason why I shouldn't move forward. What could an FBI agent do that I couldn't? I say nothing. Nothing at all.

S o, Friday afternoon, now over two weeks
since my father was first arrested, we were
off to the airport, off to save my father. I was a
kind of American hero. More important, I was
finally embarking on the kind of international luxury travel that I always believed was somehow
owed to me. This wasn't some kind of military-style
trip to Mexico where I was going to get yelled at by some beefy
drill sergeant. This was about pampering, excess, and comfort.
And as we arrived at the ticket counter, and passed easily
through the first-class line, and then made our way to the first-
class lounge, which was tastefully decorated with stained-glass
windows and hardwood paneling, I realized that I hadn't been
mistaken and that this was the kind of life I was meant to lead.

"This is the world I want to be part of," I said.

"It's an airport lounge," Ruben said. "What's the big deal?"

It occurred to me that Ruben and Erika had taken swank
trips all their lives, so what did they care? I decided I should try
to act cooler. Didn't want anyone to think I was out of place.

We took seats at a small cocktail table, unbuttoned our
coats, smiled at each other, and then greeted the woman who
arrived to take our order. Ruben and Erika each asked for a

Coke, which I almost did too. But then I thought twice and decided I should really start this whole thing off right. True, this was Seattle. But this was the Air France lounge, and this woman was French, and there's not really a drinking age in France, so I decided to try my luck.

"I'll take a glass of champagne," I said.

Erika and Ruben nervously looked away, as if to pretend they weren't with me. And the cocktail waitress too hesitated a bit. But it all passed. And in the next instant, the woman turned around and headed back to the bar to get our drinks.

Now, let me say I'm no big drinker. But I am a man of great sophistication. That's definitely true. So when I can have something like a glass of champagne, what am I supposed to do? A guy like me was meant to drink champagne in international airport lounges. The real question on my mind as the woman brought me my champagne was why I hadn't done more of this kind of thing before. The main reason, I suppose, is that I was underage, which can really prevent a guy like me from having a lot of fun in this world. But strangely, go into high-end Air France airport lounges, and they don't seem to care. I guess that's the advantage of throwing around money—people let you do what you want. Sadly, it took me a long time to discover this. Never had any real money to throw around, given the tight leash my dad kept me on. But while Dad was in jail, I was going to do lots of experimenting. Experimental behavior. Beginning at the airport. In fact, I had several glasses of champagne just to embrace the spirit of the whole thing.

"We're not even out of the U.S.," Ruben said as I asked for a third glass.

I tried to look insulted and was about to explain the joys of fine champagne when Erika kind of changed speed and said she'd actually like a glass as well. And things got even better when the champagne came. Erika took her glass, stood up, stepped over to the little two-seat couch I was sitting on, and sat very close to me. "To Paris, and to a successful mission," she said, lifting her glass in the air.

"Hear, hear," I said, and put my arm around Erika (in a friendly way—the way that I could get away with). Was good to know that I would at least have one friend who would get into the spirit of this, although Ruben kind of gave in a little and raised his glass of Coke. "To Paris," he finally said.

At any rate, we were in the airport lounge for about an hour and a half—we were there early. Finally, after another round of drinks, we were called to board the plane. I gave the lady serving us a big tip (it's always been a sort of a dream of mine to be a big tipper) and we headed off toward the gate.

So let me tell you something about champagne. It gives you a terrible headache. First, it makes you kind of drunk. Then it gives you a terrible headache. I started to feel mine just after we boarded our flight. And it really set in once I had grabbed my seat. Might seem like a lesson to me. But I say that it's just proof positive that champagne is definitely not for wimps. Have to be a man to drink champagne.

"You look like you're going to start crying," Ruben said, looking over at me as he sat down. We were next to each other in these magnificent reclining loungers that were more like beds than airplane seats. But my head was really hurting, so my seat was hard to enjoy.

I asked the stewardess for a couple of aspirin and then told Rubin to watch what he drank. "Champagne is not for amateurs," I said.

So, ordinarily, I'd have lots of things to say about the flight. Lots of funny observations. Lots of interesting little details. I'd amaze you with my insight. But, sadly, the trip was made slightly difficult by a small complication.

Like I said, I sat next to Ruben. Erika sat across the aisle from us—next to some stranger, although after having been in the air only fifteen minutes, I'd say they started to get pretty friendly. He was some young, square-jawed banker off to Paris to swing some kind of big deal. Makes me sick, really. Erika, however, bought the whole I'm-a-handsome-rich-guy thing hook, line, and sinker. Really impressed. She kept saying, "It all sounds so exciting," as he talked about his various business meetings and financial dealings.

He kept responding, "Oh, not really."

Please.

The other thing that drove me crazy was that this guy was so different from Erika's professed "type"—the tattooed young criminals she normally clung to. I mean, I always thought that it was precisely because I wasn't the tattooed type that Erika wasn't dying to go out with me. But now this joker in the suit seemed to be totally winning her over. I mean, if all it took was a suit and a fancy job, it should be no problem for me. Maybe the job thing would be hard for me to swing. But a suit. I could wear a suit. Was even planning to when we got to Paris.

I guess I shouldn't have been that worried. He was about thirty—much older than Erika—so I can't imagine she would have actually gone out with him. Illegal, even, I think. But it still upset me. I just hate it when people other than me get that kind of attention. And it was clear that the flirty thing between them just escalated as time passed, especially when she started going on about her psych books. She said something like, "I'm reading this book about group psychology. Don't you think it's amazing that big groups of people—like businesses—can find ways to work together? And each group is different. That's what amazes me."

And he said, "That's such an interesting insight. You're really perceptive about these things." Sickening.

I should say that the whole thing was highlighted by the fact that I wasn't sitting next to some beautiful French girl who wanted to "show me the sights" when we landed. As usual, I was sitting next to Ruben, who was fast asleep and drooling on himself. Story of my life. Sad but true.

S o, it's a long flight to Paris, and with the **24** time difference, we landed the next morning. How it always works, I guess. I will say that getting off the plane was kind of exciting. A new place, weird-looking buildings, strange people, etc. But we were really tired. Hard to concentrate. We made it past the border guards, though, and into the main part of the airport with relative ease. Then Ruben and I grabbed our luggage while Erika wrapped things up with the freak banker.

"It was so nice meeting you," she said. "Good luck with your meetings today."

"Have a fun time this week," he replied. Then he reached into his wallet and pulled out a business card. "Give me a call if you ever need anything. I could arrange a great summer internship at my bank if you're ever interested. In Seattle or Paris."

Great.

Anyway, they wrapped things up. We staggered out of the airport. And in the next moment, we jumped in a cab.

"Take us to the Ritz," I said in my terrible Pencrest French.

The driver just turned around and stared at me like I was out of my mind, and then he said something that I didn't understand at all. I wanted to tell him that he wasn't speaking very clearly, but I didn't know what the French for that was. Just as I was thinking of trying out his English, Erika issued an order in her much sweeter and more polished French, and in the next minute, we were on our way to the hotel.

So the Ritz is in a swank part of Paris—Place Vendôme, to be exact—where these huge, stone-columned buildings sur-round a so-called obelisk (a thin pointy thing that sticks into the sky) and beautiful people who look like models all mill about. I've really never seen anything like it, especially not in Seattle, and I could hardly believe how beautiful it all was when we pulled up to the entrance.

It was late morning when we arrived, and there were lots of people heading in and out. A man in a long coat and white gloves ran out to open the cab door and help us with our luggage. I paid the driver and then turned to follow the luggage guy up the stairs that led to the lobby. He was speaking English to us and making small talk about our flight and wishing us a pleasant stay.

"I'm so happy to have you as our guests," he said. "Where are you from?"

"Seattle," I replied.

"For a vacation? Or perhaps you have business here." This was a nice touch. We clearly weren't there on business, but it was nice for him to suggest that this was at least possible.

"Just vacation," I replied. "Spring break. It was either here or Boise. But all the nice hotels in Boise were booked."

The man just smiled and nodded at me. A very charming gentleman, really, especially because he was hefting around our bags. I like anyone who's willing to carry things for me.

The Ritz's interior is actually hard to describe, because the only way to do it involves words and phrases like "absolute best" and "most amazing." I sound like an eight-year-old girl who's just seen her favorite boy band. But the fact is that all these phrases are absolutely true. Marble floors, crystal chandeliers, brass railings, beautiful staff. Really is the "most amazing" place I've ever been.

Even Erika—linguistic genius—was reduced to this kind of thing: "This place is so awesome. I can't believe how awesome this place is."

Ruben too. He said, "I can't believe this place," about eight times, and this was before we even made it to the check-in counter.

Was nice for me to hear. As much high-toned traveling as they had done, they were still impressed by this. We were all equals now.

The check-in went smoothly. The guy had absolutely no hesitation about three kids from the United States checking into the best hotel in Paris. I guess they're used to rich kids floating through. "I am happy to welcome you to the Ritz, Mr. Macalister," the man said. "My name is Henri, and if there is anything you need, you may ask me or anyone on our staff for it."

"Thank you, my good man," I said as he handed me back my father's credit card. This was actually kind of an awkward thing for me to say—had a tinge of sarcasm about it, although I really was trying to be smooth. (Sad.) But Henri just smiled warmly, as though I had just said exactly the right thing. French hoteliers are geniuses. This is a fact.

After we got our keys, we walked with another luggage carrier, a so-called bellhop, to our rooms. The red carpets, marble statues, and fresh flowers stretched on forever. And there wasn't an elevator, staircase, or hallway that didn't make you feel like you were in the most lavish and expensive place on the planet. The rooms we booked were the same. Absolutely incredible. Thick carpet, plasma TVs, marble bathrooms, you name it. Everything a man could want. We each stepped into our own rooms alone, and in the next second we were back in the hall, all with enormous smiles on our faces.

"This place is incredible," Ruben said. "If I didn't think we were going to get killed in the next few days, I might even say I was glad to be here."

"I don't care if we do die," Erika said. "This is totally worth it. I could stay here for the rest of my life."

Then we all ran back into our rooms to check them out again. Really. Amazing. Was going to be quite a trip.

N ow, I should say at this point that I have actually done some swank things in my life. As mind-boggling as the Ritz was, it wasn't the only nice place I'd ever been. My father had a so-called standing in the community, and occasionally he'd get invited to things around Seattle where he'd be obliged to have some kind of family member in tow. But such invitations always came with strict and angry warnings: "I need you to come to this such-and-such," my dad would say, "but if you do anything stupid, I'll murder you." Yes, a bit harsh. But I do a lot of stupid things. Have all my life. So he wasn't totally out of order.

I'd say that part of the reason my dad was also kind of tough on me on these occasions was that he didn't like them much either. My father was always mistrustful of people with too much money. To a certain extent, I don't even think he ever really saw himself as a bona fide rich man, although that's clearly what he was. I think being from northern Minnesota— Duluth, of all places—made him feel like he was never really part of the club.

I will say that my mother dying had something to do with his paranoia. He's always been kind of a crazy and paranoid guy.

25

But my mother could really work a room. She was really something in social situations, although she wasn't at all any sort of
phony social climber. She was a doctor and had the same
brains my dad did. But people liked her. A lot. She was confi-
dent and comfortable in any social situation, and I think it
made life easier on my father. I have to admit that I wasn't
really aware of all this when my mother died but kind of figured
some of it out about five months after I lost her. It was
Christmastime, and I had to go to this high-end party that MRI
threw every year. Families were always invited, although this
was the first time I had come. I think my dad thought I should
stay home from this one too but then reconsidered. I think he
wanted to keep up appearances, as they say. And since his
employees were bringing along wives and kids, he decided he
should do the same.

Now, I was eleven years old and just entering the height of
my charming and cute mischievous phase. The party was at a
really nice hotel in downtown Seattle called the Fairmont, and
the catering was over the top. Smoked salmon, shrimp, champagne, the works. They had also wheeled in upright video
games and a virtual reality setup to amuse the kids. Anyway, I
had had a bit too much sugar, and there was this girl I was kind
of flirting with (and by flirting, I mean playing tag). I tagged her,
and then she tagged me, and in the next instant we were kind
of darting through the crowd to the center of the ballroom,
where this humungous ice sculpture sat in the middle of a table

covered with food and punch bowls. Now, you'd imagine that they'd put such things on a sturdy table. A very sturdy table. And if you think about it, the whole thing wasn't even my fault. But it's true that I wanted to tag this girl, and it's true that I kind of lunged at her in a place where no one ought to be lunging, and before I knew what had happened, I had knocked over the table—ice sculpture and all—and was lying facedown on the ground, covered in punch and salmon, wondering where I was.

I was, however, quickly returned to reality. A huge hand grabbed me by the wrist and hoisted me up and walked me out of the ballroom and into a small empty room at the other end of the corridor. It was hard to see what was going on. I was still kind of in shock. But I rightly assumed that the mysterious hand and the powerful force whisking me away was my father, and the next thing I knew, he and I were in a darkened conference room and he was reading me the riot act. Was really terrible. He was really mad. About as mad as I've ever seen him. Furious. But it only lasted for a few minutes. He was pissed, and my dad can yell for hours on end. But a few minutes into the yelling, he just kind of halted, like he was searching for what to say next—desperately searching—and then, suddenly, he started to cry.

It was really shocking. I had never seen this kind of thing before. When my mother died, he pretty much hid everything. Or he just looked shell-shocked, like someone had just exploded a bomb next to him. Totally stunned. But I never saw him cry like that. I never saw him break down this way. Even at the funeral, he only shed a few manly tears. No breakdowns. It was actually kind of frightening.

Anyway, the sobbing came and then the apologies. He said he never wanted me to see him like this. And then he cried some more and said that he just didn't think he was going to cut it alone and that he didn't think he could raise me right.

"I just don't think I can handle this," he kept saying through his tears. And the more he said it, the more I kept thinking about what a rotten son I was and how I wished I hadn't knocked that table over. And then I started crying too because it was all just so strange and frightening.

Anyway, my father and I stood there for about five minutes sobbing and wondering if there would ever be an end to this. The fact was that it seemed that there wouldn't be. We were crying for my mother, and whatever pact we could come up with—however good I agreed to be, and however tolerant my dad promised to be—it wasn't going to bring her back, and in the end, that's what we were crying about. Not the stupid table or the stupid ice sculpture.

All very painful. But the tears dried, as they always do, and when we were back in control, I told my dad I was sorry for knocking over the table. And he said that he was sorry he got so mad but that he'd need my help in the future. "This is very hard on both of us," he said. "But we've got to act like men. We've got to hold it together. I know I'm not always the most sensitive father. I want to be. I want to be that kind of father. But I need you to watch yourself from now on. This is very, very hard on both of us, and we need to be careful."

I agreed. I said I'd be good. And I meant it. When I was saying that, I wasn't lying. Or I didn't think I was. I didn't mean to. I have to say that looking back on it now, I feel a bit guilty, though. I mean, I absolutely did not stay out of trouble. I was no help to my father at all. I was nothing but an aggravation.

But I wasn't the only one to go back on my promise. The day after the party, my dad seemed to soften, seemed to be a bit more open around me. But as time went on—in just a few weeks, in fact—he was back to his old self. Closed off. Hardened. Silent. Sour. A hard-ass nearly-seventy-year-old tough guy who seemed totally confused and scandalized by me.

Anyway, all relationships are a two-way street. Can't blame him and I can't blame myself, entirely. But it was a disappointment. The whole thing was a disappointment. I was disappointed with myself and I was disappointed with my father. I mean, who'd think that two family members could be so awkward around each other? Anyway, I don't really know what else to say.

T hat said, back to the Ritz.

26

After running around our rooms for a few minutes, we went outside for a walk and to find something to eat. We were hungry. However, more than being hungry, we were suddenly dead tired. Dead tired. We had missed a night of sleep, after all, due to the flight and the time change. So even though we had plans for an elaborate lunch served to us by some kind of snobby French waiter, we actually just went to a small grocery store and bought candy bars and a couple of boxes of cookies.

"This isn't what I thought my first French meal would be," Erika said. "But I'm so tired, I don't think I care."

After buying the food, we headed back to our rooms. It was nap time. Frankly, after I had stuffed a few cookies into my mouth on the street, I didn't even think I had the strength to push the elevator button back in the hotel. But I managed. And in the next instant I was crashed out on my four-hundred-dollar-a-night bed, surrounded by candy bar wrappers and cookie crumbs. Kind of paradise, really.

We were up again in about five hours—at about 6 p.m., or 9 a.m. Seattle time. And when Ruben and Erika came in my room—I was the last one up—they were all smiles and ready for fun.

"Let's go, rock star," Ruben said. "Time to go have some fun."

I was still kind of groggy. "Is that Ruben telling me to go have fun?" I finally said. "I must be dreaming."

Then Erika jumped on my bed and started poking me. Kind of enjoyable, although I think she was trying to be annoying.

"Wake up, Evan," she said. "Time to get dinner and hit the clubs."

I didn't need too much persuasion. I got up quickly enough and in another minute I was in the shower. Frankly, it was pretty exciting. Foreign country and all that. And we had decided that we wouldn't do any business till the next day. I guess it sounds a little stupid now. We did have a mission to accomplish. Freeing my dad and me staying out of jail were at stake. But we had decided that we needed to play our cards right in contacting Lubchenko and that it was best to go to Café Saint-Beauvais during the day, when it might be less busy and easier to nose around. That was our reasoning, anyway. Probably we were just excited to hang around in Paris before we had to start worrying about getting ourselves killed.

Anyway, we all got cleaned up and then headed out. I suppose (for the sake of accuracy) that I should also tell you that Ruben and I were wearing suits and ties. This was something we had decided on when we were in Seattle. We figured it was a good idea since we'd be out on the town in a bustling foreign capital. I can't say Ruben looked very good in his suit. It was a bit small on him, and the jacket didn't really hang right on his shoulders.

"I'm not sure you've got that suit on right," I told Ruben as we left the Ritz and walked out onto the Place Vendôme. "You look like your mother dressed you."

"He does not," Erika quickly said, who sometimes didn't appreciate my good-hearted teasing. Still, she was laughing. Ruben was too, although he started straightening out his tie.

I should also say that I, on the other hand, looked absolutely fantastic. Really. I was like a movie star. "I look like a movie star," I said several times.

Erika and Ruben rolled their eyes at me, and Erika even stepped over and punched me on the arm. But it was true. I was very, very handsome in my suit. You wouldn't believe it.

So, the first place we went to was near the Seine, which is the big river that goes through Paris. As rivers go, it's not bad. Not quite the size of the Mississippi, but pretty big. And pretty beautiful. The place was called the Argost. It was an upscale bar that I read about in one of the guides I bought. It was listed as a "great place to see and be seen," which sounded good to me. We went in and sat down at a low table surrounded by plush red velvet chairs, and when the man came to take our orders, I asked for a vodka martini with olives. (Have I mentioned that France doesn't really have a drinking age?) Erika ordered the same. And Ruben, not to be outdone, asked for one too.

"I'll help you out with it if you run into trouble," I said.

"Listen, Evan," Ruben replied. "I hate to say this, but when I'm an investment banker, this is the life I'm going to lead all the time. You're still going to be failing algebra tests and I'm going to be a big-time deal maker, spending my evenings in Parisian bars sipping cocktails."

"Wrong," I said. "I'm dropping out of high school to become a movie star. Just look at me. And then you're going to be begging to come hang with me in L.A."

Again, Ruben and Erika laughed at me, although I really wasn't joking.

Anyway, there was some more happy teasing. And then the martinis came.

Now, let me just say at this point that it would injure me deeply if anyone thought that this was some kind of account of a teenager's booze fest in a foreign country. As I've said, I am not a big drinker, and I'm really nothing close to what might be considered a party animal. But sit down in a beautiful bar where a mustachioed man in a white dinner jacket asks, "What does monsieur desire?" and you'd feel like a fool ordering a ginger ale. It was like high-end, jet-set peer pressure, and I was a victim. It was worse than being called a baby by the captain of the rugby team when you refuse a shot of tequila. Really. (And I've had that happen.) When that man in the white jacket takes your order, you've got to ask for something expensive and potent or you feel entirely disgraced.

However, despite the pressure, I can't say I minded.

Anyway, like I said, the martinis came, and in case you've never had one, let me describe it. Next time you get a shot from the doctor, pay attention to the rubbing alcohol they put on your arm before sticking in the needle. This is basically what a martini smells like. And I imagine it would taste the same if you were to lick the rubbing alcohol off your arm before the doctor gave you the shot (although I don't know why anyone would want to do this). At any rate, a martini is a terrible drink. Really bad. And were I not such a victim of modern masculine stereotypes, I would have returned it and asked for a wine cooler. But I'm a tough guy. An international man of mystery. So I choked it down. And then I ordered another. As did Ruben. Erika, however, who was clearly much smarter than either of her male companions, ordered a Coke the second time around.

Next we went out to dinner at an expensive restaurant called the Quinze-Cinq, also not far from the river. It was fun, happy, expensive, swank—everything Paris has to offer—but definitely the most eventful moment was when I stood up from my chair to head to the men's room and bumped into a waiter who was passing behind me. Three plates covered with some kind of strange-looking French meat fell to the ground, and I had to spend the next twenty minutes apologizing, mostly using Erika as a translator.

When a French waiter yells at you, by the way, it sounds like this: "*Ehhnveequoooik suiiiiiitiiquo uuunnnnenhhnquaa aakuuuuu-*

unqueee suiiiiiitiiquooo niiikuuunnnnniiiiiii." What this means, I have no idea, but Erika kept telling him how sorry and stupid I was.

"He's very sorry and very stupid," she kept saying.

And I said these things too, although in less-perfect French. Still, I have no idea what the waiter said in response. Of course, I'm still not convinced the whole thing was actually my fault. But the waiter sure thought so. I thought he was going to punch me. But I guess he thought better of it. I probably looked a bit too tough to mess with. The tough-guy American. That was me.

Next we went to a nightclub, or "disco," as the cabdriver kept calling it. It was called Le Grenouille. This place was a bit cooler than the other venues we had been to that night, since it was filled with people our age or people closer to our age. Late teens, early twenties, I think.

Unfortunately, Ruben and I were the only guys in suits. Everyone else had on jeans and T-shirts. But that was everyone else's problem, not ours. Could we help it if French kids were slobs? But Le Grenouille was a good time. We danced, sprawled out on couches, drank beer, and listened to deafening French house music. And to make things more intriguing, I couldn't help but feel like things were kind of flirty with Erika. When we first sat down at our table, she sat up close to me on the couch, saying, "You're brave to be saving your father like this, Evan."

I agreed, of course, and then, without explanation, she threw her arms around me and jumped up on my lap.

"Promise to take care of me when the shooting starts?" she said.

Needless to say, I promised. "Don't worry about anything, sweetheart."

But she didn't spend the whole time on my lap. Was just a momentary thing. And sometimes she didn't even stay there with Ruben and me. Like, other times these freak French men would come up and ask her to dance, and then I'd have to watch her out on the dance floor with some goon who was try- ing to steal my woman. Still, Erika didn't seem to be letting any of the French dudes have more than one dance each before returning to Ruben and me. That was comforting, and brings me to one small point that I need to add at this juncture.

So, I know I often put on this conceited act, but having been rejected by as many women as I have, I think I have a pretty honest opinion of my power over the opposite sex. It's pretty minimal. Pretty sad. Still, once in a while a woman will like me. Once in a while. Must be because I have such a winning per- sonality. Babes always say they go for that kind of thing. Whatever. Erika and I got along really well. And I don't think I was imagining the flirtiness that night.

Anyway, we stayed at the club for some time before finally calling it a night. It was pretty late by this point. Well after 3 a.m., and Ruben was starting to get cranky.

"I need my bed," he started saying. Erika and I teased him a lit- tle, but the truth was that we were pretty beat too. (I was, at least.)

As we left Le Grenouille and hopped in a cab, I kept thinking about how much fun I'd had with Erika that night. I guess I shouldn't have been surprised, being in Paris and all. Still, it was nice. And as we got out of the cab and walked slowly toward the enormous front doors of the Ritz, Erika grabbed my arm and said, "I can't make it. I'm too tired." And she kept hold of me as we walked through the lobby and hopped on the elevator. Again, kind of nice. Still, I didn't know what to do because, frankly, I'm an idiot. I will say, however, that as the evening ended and we all said good night outside our rooms, I couldn't help but notice that Erika seemed a bit reluctant to let us go. But it was late—now close to 4 a.m.—and I wasn't sure quite what to say. I mean, I was thinking, *Why don't you stay in here tonight, sweetheart?* But this seemed (rightly) just a little crass. Besides, I'm not capable of making such a suggestion. Even after several martinis. So it was irrelevant, and after a strange pause, Erika just said good night. She hugged Ruben. Then she hugged me. And then (I don't think I imagined this) she gave me a little kiss on my cheek.

"See you boys in the morning," she said as she opened her door.

"Good night," Ruben said, yawning.

"Good night," I said, now opening my own door. And in the next minute I was in my hotel room, lying faceup on my bed, too tired to even take off my clothes.

27

We slept late the next morning but managed to catch the tail end of breakfast at the hotel at around eleven-thirty. We were a bit hung over, which I guess is what happens when you drink martinis, so none of us was too chipper. In fact, we all kind of sat in silence as we ate our "English-style" breakfast, which by my estimation was really an "American-style" breakfast—bacon and eggs, toast, juice, etc. If that's not American, I don't know what is.

Despite how beat we were, however, we did manage to talk about plans for that day. Clubbing had been great. And flirting with Erika was pretty cool too. Still, I think that all of us realized that we had to get down to business. Had to try to contact Lubchenko.

The day's task wasn't too complicated. I had found the address of Café Saint-Beauvais before I came down to breakfast. The plan was basically to go into the café, ask the owner or manager if they knew someone named Lubchenko (insisting that it was a matter of life and death), and hope the guy could tell us something useful. Not a sophisticated plan. But what else was there to do?

"I'll tell you who would know exactly what to do," Ruben

said as we were discussing this. "The FBI. They'd already be questioning Lubchenko by now if we had come clean."

"You'd also be in jail," I replied, cramming two pieces of bacon in my mouth. "Anyway, where's your spirit of adventure? We just flew to Paris and went out all night to the best clubs in the world. Getting hold of this Lubchenko guy and saving my father will be no problem at all."

Ruben and Erika kind of looked at each other and rolled their eyes.

"I wish I was so optimistic," Ruben said.

We decided to hit the café mid-afternoon, when we figured it would be quieter, and for the next few hours we just kind of wandered around Paris. Got a chance to see the city in the daylight. I will now record the following four observations about this nation:

First, French people are among the strangest on the planet. They are an unwashed bunch, oddly dressed, kind of dreamy, and not at all the kind of energetic (neurotic) people you would find at, say, MRI. Second, every building is a breathtaking work of art. We saw a lot that afternoon when we were killing time— the Opera, the Eiffel Tower, the Trocadero, etc., etc., etc. All places you'll find in any tourist guide, and all places worth fighting the tourists to see. Really incredible. But I was more blown away by the fact that even little, unimportant buildings that weren't one bit famous were kind of mind-blowing. Everything seemed to be a combination of ancient stone, wooden beams, simple white plaster, and ornate ironwork. You kind of felt that even if you lived in the worst building in Paris, you'd still be living like a king. Third, French drivers are the worst in the world. I have not been everywhere in the world, but I'm sure this is true. I very nearly died eight times just that day, and each time all I was doing was standing on the sidewalk. Fourth, run-of-the-mill French food—the junk you'll find at any street corner butcher or bakery—is better than anything you can find in Seattle or anywhere in the United States and probably the world. I think this is why French people are so sleepy-headed and mealy-brained. If you're constantly stuffing exquisite pastries in your mouth, there's no reason to get too excited about anything. How I felt when I was eating an éclair or a hot crepe smeared with Nutella and bananas. The world could be ending and I wouldn't care one way or another. I'd just be thinking about what was going on in my mouth.

Anyway, I guess there's more to say about France. But I don't want to get too distracted.

So, Café Saint-Beauvais was in a pretty nice neighborhood (the so-called Seventh Arrondissement) on the other side of the river from the Ritz. I should point out that a café in France is basically a big restaurant kind of place that serves coffee, liquor, and food pretty much all day and all night long. Most cafés have outdoor seating because French people go bananas over fresh air and sunshine. But cafés come in many different shapes and sizes, and I have to say that the Saint-Beauvais was on the nicer end of the spectrum. Still, it wasn't very big and showy. You could definitely walk down the street and not really think much of it. But it also wasn't small. It had a biggish main room, and there were about ten tables outside. All irrelevant, I guess. Point is that after walking around for a few hours, looking into stores and staring at the freak people that walked by, we arrived at our destination. And after a few minutes of sweating what was next, we walked in.

It was decided that Erika would do the talking since my French sucked and hers was good. And the fact that she's attractive helped. Apparently, that kind of thing goes over well in Paris.

As we entered, a waiter walked by us, and Erika turned, about to ask if he could direct us to the manager. But just then, an older man came through the kitchen door and walked behind the bar. This was probably the guy to ask. Looked like he was in charge.

Approaching this guy was actually kind of nerve-racking, and in those ten brief steps it took to get to the bar, it kind of dawned on me what we were doing. I mean, even if Lubchenko was some kind of angel, he was still involved in enough bad-guy stuff to have evidence against Colburn and possibly Mr. Richmond in a murder case. I didn't know how Erika felt, but when I first heard her speak, I could tell she was a bit nervous as well, since her voice kind of cracked.

"Excuse me, sir," she said, kind of weakly.

(Obviously the conversation was in French and this is only a rough translation.)

"Yes?" he said, only half looking up. He had a clipboard in his hand and was focusing on a big page of numbers.

"I was wondering if you could help us with something."

The man paused, put his clipboard aside, and looked up at us more carefully. He smiled, though, when he saw us, and I have to say it was a pretty friendly smile. Not the smile of some crook trying to pull something over on you. In fact, in general, the guy seemed like any mild-mannered citizen of a free city. His sandy brown hair was neatly combed. He had glasses hanging off the end of his nose. And he was sporting a sweater that you might see Mr. Rogers wearing on TV.

"Of course," he said, after looking us over a bit more.

"We were wondering if you knew a man who goes by the name of Lubchenko."

The expression on the man's face barely changed at all. The smile stayed. The teeth were still exposed. The lips didn't tremble at all. Almost nothing. Almost. But there was just the trace of some tiny little twinkle that came to his eyes as Erika said "Lubchenko." A tiny flash of surprise that went away as soon as it came. Then, after what seemed to me like a very long pause, he said, "I'm very sorry, mademoiselle, but I have never heard of this man."

Erika paused and looked at me. Why, I don't know. I didn't know what to say. "Are you sure?" Erika finally said, looking back at the man. "It's very important. It's a matter of life and death."

The man kept smiling and then said, "I would help you if I could, but I do not know this man at all."

Erika paused again for a second and then said, "Are you the owner?"

"Yes, in a manner of speaking," he replied. "But I don't know everything. Maybe this man comes here. But I don't know who he is. I'm very sorry, but I have never heard of him."

Then, according to plan, Erika said, "If this man does turn up here, if you do happen to meet him, will you tell him that we came to see him and that we're staying at the Ritz until Wednesday?" (It was Sunday at that point.) Erika then produced a small business card we'd snagged from the hotel and wrote our room numbers on the back. "It's very important," she continued. "It's about MRI and Mr. Emil Belachek." She then wrote the words *MRI* and *Belachek* above our room numbers.

The man smiled again and said, "If such a person appears at Café Saint-Beauvais, I will give this to him. But I do not know him myself, so I hope you won't be disappointed if I cannot help you."

"We understand," Erika said. She thanked the man, Ruben and I did the same, and then we headed out the door.

We walked for about a block before we started talking, but when we started, it was a kind of flurry of giggling and choppy sentences. For some reason, even though absolutely nothing had happened, the whole thing was pretty intense. We all agreed that it was impossible to tell if the guy was lying to us or not. But we each kind of suspected that he knew something. "Just the way his eyes flickered when he heard 'Lubchenko,'" Ruben said. "Still, if he knows something and doesn't tell us, we're in the same position as before. I mean, I don't think we can beat it out of him, for instance."

"This is true," I said, as I looked down at my embarrassingly thin biceps. "But we still have a shot at finding something out. I mean, he might talk it over with Lubchenko and give us a call. He does have our address now."

"He just seemed like such a nice man," Erika said. "Not a spy type."

To this we all agreed, although it was clear that niceness didn't always mean that much. "Mr. Richmond seems like a nice guy too," I said. "And who knows what he's been up to?"

This was, in fact, an issue I had been thinking about more and more.

28

S o, the fact was that I had been giving a lot of thought to the Mr. Richmond thing. Not careful, methodical analysis. It just kept popping into my mind—that he might be involved in this. Obviously, Lubchenko had mentioned him as a possibility in his e-mail. And since Colburn was almost certainly involved, it seemed even more likely. Colburn was, after all, Mr. Richmond's right-hand man. It was just so hard to get my mind around the idea. He was a nice guy. That was true. And he was nice to me. The fact is that in some ways I really looked up to him—I even wanted my dad to be more like him. But he was kind of strange as well.

Anyway, here are a couple of examples of experiences I had with Mr. Richmond, both of which kept coming to mind after everything went down with my father.

About four years earlier, Mr. Richmond threw this big barbecue at his house for higher-level employees at the company. A totally deluxe occasion. His enormous house was decorated to the hilt. His pool was sparkling and eighty degrees. There was a live band, eighteen different kinds of roasted meat, and another ice sculpture (which I carefully avoided).

Anyway, I was kind of walking around with my plate of ribs and listening to the music when Mr. Richmond approached me and asked me if I wanted to see his new game room.

"I just had it redone, Evan," he said. "You're going to love it."

"All right," I said. "Sure." (What else did I have to do?)

We went into the house, through his gigantic kitchen, along a hall that went behind his dining room, and into what seemed like a rich man's arcade—high ceilings, fireplace, side bar, and jam-packed with every kind of game you can imagine. He had a Foosball table, a pool table, a Ping-Pong table, three old-school video game machines (Pac-Man, Mortal Kombat, and Defender), an ancient pinball machine, and a million other way-expensive toys. It was really something.

"Want to play Pac-Man?" he asked.

"All right," I said. It was an old game, but I was pretty sure I could waste him.

"Hang on for a second," he said, and walked behind the wooden bar at the side of the room and grabbed a beer out of the fridge. Then he stopped for a moment. "How old are you, Evan?" he asked.

"I'm twelve," I replied. (I was twelve when this went down.)

He paused for a second and then said, "Want a beer?"

"Sure," I replied. Seemed outrageous, but why not?

He popped another beer open and walked it over to me. "Don't tell your dad about this," he said.

"Don't worry about that," I replied.

Then he flipped a special switch at the side of the game, and we were in round one of Pac-Man.

We stayed down there for about fifteen minutes. We played two games, and I crushed him both times. To be expected. I was a twelve-year-old. The whole time, I was sipping on my Budweiser and wondering if my dad was going to suddenly come in and bust me. Fortunately, he didn't arrive, and I finished the beer under the careful supervision of Mr. Richmond, who kept saying things like, "How's that taste, big guy?" and, "You ever had a beer before?"

I just kind of smiled the whole time, saying I liked the beer and looking over my shoulder for my dad.

I don't know. From the outside, it might not seem that monumental. It was just a beer. But I was only twelve. And I've got to admit, I was kind of in awe of this guy. I mean, he had real live stand-up video games in his house. The whole place was like some kind of playground. And he let me drink a beer with him. Have to say that for me (for me as my twelve-year-old self), it was a pretty revolutionary moment. Kind of had a revelatory vision of what I wanted my life to be like.

A similar thing happened a few years later that fits in with this. We were driving home from another company event. It was a golf-and-country-club outing this time that included a big family picnic. I was fourteen at the time, and Mr. Richmond was giving my father and me a ride home afterward. We were in his brand-new BMW, which I think must have cost about eighteen million dollars. This was one incredible car. Really something.

Anyway, I got to sit in the front seat because my dad wanted to sit in the back so he could talk on his cell phone with about a thousand pieces of paper spread out beside him. So Mr. Richmond and I were talking and chatting about this and that, and I finally said, "This car is absolutely amazing."

I was just being polite. Just making small talk. But Mr. Richmond smirked, looked sideways at me for a second, and then suddenly pulled over. "You want to drive it?" he said.

At this point, my dad pulled the cell phone away from his ear and said, "Absolutely not."

Mr. Richmond looked over the seat and laughed. "C'mon, Evan Senior," he said. "If he hits anything, I'll pay for it."

"Out of the question," Dad replied.

"Lighten up. It's just a car."

"Evan, you're not to drive this car."

Now, these guys were business partners, so they supposedly got along great. But I have to say it was a bit tense. There was a bit of a power struggle here. Nothing too serious, maybe. But this really was a case of their different philosophies clashing. They were a dynamite business team—my dad was the steady scholar, and Mr. Richmond was the well-groomed salesman. Now their worlds were suddenly colliding over whether or not a fourteen-year-old kid should drive a brand-new BMW. I don't know. Maybe this kind of clash happened more often than I thought. But it was the first time I'd ever seen it so close up.

The problem was that the way things spun out, it was left up to me to resolve it. Mr. Richmond looked at me, looked at my father, then said, "Let's let the kid decide." Then he stepped out of the car, leaving the keys dangling in the ignition.

I got out of the car too, not sure what I was doing, and as I took my position in the driver's seat and Mr. Richmond took the passenger seat, my father said, "You're not to drive this car, Evan."

Now, any kid knows that the dad always trumps this situation. And with my dad, that was doubly true because he was such a maniac. And the first thing that crossed my mind was, *Well, this would have been fun.* But I was feeling a little pissy that evening. Kind of tired of my dad for all the usual reasons. And I'll tell you something else: We were at an event that was supposed to be fun, was supposed to include families, but he totally ditched me all day. Had to talk business. I was nothing more than a prop. A requirement listed on the invitation: *Bring family.* And to top it all off, on the drive home, he was still working. He was sitting in that backseat surrounded by papers and talking on his cell phone like we had spent the day at his office. Whatever. Maybe I'm just rationalizing this. But in the next second, I turned on the engine and pulled onto the road.

Now, I should point out that I had very little sense of how to drive. I knew the basics—what I had figured out from watching other people and from the few times I'd driven Ruben's parents' car up and down their driveway. Really, not that much practice. Still, I wasn't bad, and I managed to take it about a mile before we entered a more-populated area and I thought I should pull over. And it was really pretty fun. Not many fourteen-year-olds get to drive a brand-new BMW.

During this brief hurrah, my dad remained silent. He had lots of ways to play this kind of situation. In this case, it was a matter of testing me, watching me fail, and reserving the screaming for later. Mr. Richmond was in the car, after all. And my dad (on some occasions) believes in a certain kind of dignity. So he shut up. But it was pretty clear that he was furious.

Anyway, Mr. Richmond tried to start up the conversation after he took the wheel again. Kept saying things like, "See, no harm done," and, "The world didn't end."

I just sat there wondering how these two had made it this far together. The truth is that they really did need each other. Still, their partnership was kind of astonishing when you think about it.

But I actually was not thinking much about it by this point. I had other things on my mind. My dad was fuming. I had my back to him, but he was fuming. Didn't even make any more phone calls. And when we pulled up to the house, he didn't move. He just said, "Evan, go inside."

This seemed like a good time for me to do as I was told. He stayed in the car with Mr. Richmond for about ten minutes. What they said, I don't know. And by the time my dad came in, I didn't really care. He opened the door screaming, and for the next half an hour I listened to him scream about all the things he always screamed about—my grades, my future, my lack of discipline, my willful disobedience. Anyway, TV was cut off for a month, I was not to have any dessert during that time, and I would have to write a five-page essay on the importance of obeying our nation's laws, "Specifically the law that involves the driving age," he said, pounding his fist on his desk.

Actually pissed me off. I mean, how much could this guy punish me? A five-page paper for my dad? I wanted to kill myself. But I guess I didn't have much choice. My dad had plenty of other ways to make life tough on me. (Like forbidding me to see Erika, for instance.)

But I will say this one last thing. I hate to do it, but I feel obligated. For the record, I have to say that there's almost nothing I've ever done that has made me feel as bad as driving Mr. Richmond's car that day. I had plenty of good reasons for driving it. I really did. Just one afternoon with my dad and anyone would want to rebel. But I kind of sold him out for Mr. Richmond. I should have taken his side, even if he was being unfair and even if he was a boring prig who never let me do anything. I should have dealt with that matter some other time. I don't know. I can name a hundred times that I felt like my dad sold me out. It's not like he ever told Mr. Cippiloni to stuff it when he called home about an algebra test.

Whatever. Point is that I felt bad. And I've got to say that for as cush a life as Mr. Richmond had and for as much as I wished my dad was more like him, it was kind of slimy of him to pull what he did. He shouldn't have done that to my father, and he shouldn't have done that to me. That was no position to put me in.

Anyway, I'm not sure that I've gotten any closer to describing my feelings about Mr. Richmond here. I've made things a bit more complicated, maybe. But this was a complicated issue. And the truth is that none of this probably had anything to do with anything. Giving a kid a beer and letting him drive your car are completely different from strangling a guy over weapons of mass destruction. Still, as Ruben, Erika, and I kicked around Paris, the idea of Mr. Richmond being involved in killing Belachek and framing my father kept popping into my head, and it was so depressing that I almost didn't know what to do.

And the stories I just told reminded me of other things as well—things that had been on my mind the whole time. I thought about that car thing quite a bit. I thought about my dad sitting in jail in Seattle and me holding on to the one piece of evidence that might get him out and felt pretty bad. I mean, doing the right thing is always complicated, and I wasn't exactly sure where I stood. I wasn't even sure I was completely wrong to drive the BMW that day. I guess I just felt bad that things were so rotten between us. I mean, I had already concluded lots of times in my life that I couldn't really count on my father for too much support. But the real question I had after he had been arrested was how much he could count on me. That was what troubled me the most. I guessed I'd be able to answer this question a bit better in the next week—if we found Lubchenko. A lot of pressure.

29

Anyway, back to Paris.

The visit to Café Saint-Beauvais had been discouraging. The man with the little glimmer in his eye said he knew nothing. But what could we expect? Even if this café owner dude was down with Lubchenko, it was hardly likely that he'd just point him out to us. We were three complete strangers. So despite walking back to the Ritz empty-handed, we stayed upbeat.

"I bet we get a call from Lubchenko by the end of the day," Erika said. "And if not, we still have other options."

Erika then suggested that we check the Parisian phone book for the name Lubchenko. Why not? Seemed as good an idea as any. We all agreed that Lubchenko was probably not the guy's real name. Belachek used aliases, after all. But we were desperate. Did not want to have to go to the FBI with the stolen laptop. Nope. And it wasn't going to hurt to look it up.

Back at the hotel, we each grabbed the phone books in our room and sat on my bed. Not that difficult. Just looked under *L*. Sadly, however, there was absolutely nothing under *Lubchenko*. After looking at the residential listings, we went through the business section, trying to find anything that might have the name on it. We actually went page by page for this one. Took a couple of hours. But again, nothing.

"I think we need a good, stiff drink," I said as we reached the end of that task. Erika and Ruben stared blankly at me. "Okay. Maybe not," I continued. "But I'm not sure guys like Lubchenko are listed in things like the phone book. Did anyone look under *spy* yet? What about *underworld figures*?"

"Okay, Evan," Erika said. "Maybe we can cut the sarcasm bit. I mean, I don't even know why I'm here with you guys. I'm not the one that was stealing office equipment."

This was a good point.

We sat there for a little while longer, still flipping through the phone books, and then I suggested another small plan. It wasn't much, actually, but it was an idea. I was thinking it might be worth our while to go back to the Saint-Beauvais and check it out a bit more. We wouldn't go in. But maybe we'd hang around outside, maybe down the street a bit, where we wouldn't be seen.

"A stakeout," I said. "Like on *Starsky and Hutch*. We might see something."

The problem, of course, was that such a stakeout takes a lot of time, and you've got to be hidden. International spies who know someone's watching their hideout will rarely go there. Also, what were we looking for? It wasn't likely that Lubchenko would show up in a black SUV surrounded by bodyguards. He probably looked like anyone else. Still, what did we have to lose? It beat sitting around and waiting for Lubchenko to honor us with a phone call.

Anyway, after a little discussion, Ruben and Erika agreed. And then Ruben suggested something else.

"Let's check online," he said. "The Ritz has a little office center with computer terminals. We can search for *Lubchenko* and *Paris.*"

"Sounds good to me," Erika said.

I agreed, although I wasn't too excited. Ruben and I had looked for Lubchenko online before, and nothing seemed very important. Although we didn't exactly know what we were looking for. Again, guys like Lubchenko were rarely listed in ways that might indicate that they were international spies. Still, we took another shot.

So, Lubchenko is a more common name than you'd think, although it definitely wasn't Parisian, and it definitely wasn't French. This made things easy once we got online and began searching. If we were looking online for *Lubchenko* in Eastern Europe, there'd be like three million entries. But amazingly, there were only a few entries under the key words *Lubchenko* and *Paris*. And actually, they didn't even point to Paris. They pointed to a suburb called Champlan—outside the area of the phone books. Apparently there was a service station called Lubchenko Auto. It wasn't much, but it was the only relevant listing.

"Lubchenko's a mechanic?" Ruben said.

"Could be a front," Erika said.

All very puzzling. But we at least had something new on our plate—a trip to Champlan.

But it was evening by the time we found the garage online, and we decided to put the journey off till the next day. The plan at that moment was to head back to the Saint-Beauvais and check it out a bit more. And then back to the clubs.

"No more clubs," Ruben said. "I need sleep."

"You can sleep when you get back to Seattle," I said.

"I need sleep," he said again.

"No sleep," Erika replied.

So the Saint-Beauvais was only about a fifteen-minute walk from the hotel. We were all a bit hungry when we headed out, but we thought we could just pick something up after we scoped out the area. It actually turned out well that we didn't eat anything ahead of time because there was a small Chinese restaurant called Tien-Fu that was kitty-corner from the Saint-Beauvais. Seemed it would be a great lookout post for us. Not only was it close, but it also had a tiny seating area on the second floor. It was a perfect spot to grab a table, kick back, get some chow, and watch for terrorists.

So by Ritz standards, this restaurant was way cheap, and after we were seated by the upstairs window and had a good view of the Saint-Beauvais, we ordered half the menu. It was really kind of sick how much food we got. But we'd probably be there for a while. At least for a few hours. So we needed lots of food to keep us going.

We did, in fact, stay there for about three hours. We ate sweet-and-sour pork, vegetable dumplings, shrimp toast, mu shu chicken, spareribs, and a million other things, the whole time staring out the window and talking about whatever came to mind. It was actually fairly pleasant to be honest.

"I think I like being on a stakeout as much as clubbing," I said as I squeezed the contents of an egg roll onto my plate.

"I'm just happy no one's trying to get me to drink a martini," Erika said, staring at me.

"Me too," Ruben added.

"Later," I said. "Later."

Anyway, for as relaxed as it was, the stakeout wasn't very productive. We saw a million people go in and out of the Saint-Beauvais, but no one that looked like an international spy. And what such a spy would look like was also a mystery. Still, we decided that this whole thing wasn't such a bad idea. And we tried our best to remember what people looked like. We decided that we'd come back. Repeat customers might be a signal of something, although we had no idea of what. And by the time we were ready to pack it in, none of us felt like we had completely wasted our time. We had eaten well. And we had made friends with our waiter, who was this really young guy who was trying to grow a beard. It was definitely not working. A terrible, mangy, ridiculous beard. But he was nice, and he never tried to kick us out, although the restaurant wasn't very busy, so they really had no need for our table.

Still, as we walked home and assessed the day, we also had to conclude that we had come up with very little. Nothing, really. And when we got back to the hotel and discovered that there was no message from anyone named Lubchenko, we realized again that the day had really been kind of a wash.

Still, it could have been worse. "At least no one tried to kill us," Erika said as we got onto the elevator.

We all agreed that it was, in fact, a good thing that no one tried to kill us. And we still had a night on the town ahead of us. It was late—by real-life standards. It was now after eleven. But any international traveler knows that that's just when clubs start to get going. So we were right on schedule.

"No," Ruben said. "No. No more clubs. Not for me." But he was a little more perky after all that food. The color had come back to his cheeks. And he was smiling. And when we got to our rooms, we agreed to meet up after showers, a change of clothes, and a little primping.

It's hard trying to figure out what to do from a guidebook. But after about ten minutes, I picked a spot that looked good. It was called Cité and was supposedly where kids of the Paris elite hung out. *Young people run wild,* the guide said. *A place that teenage kids of movie stars and politicians call home.* Perfect for us. Just the kind of place where we'd fit in. It did, however, warn about long lines at the velvet rope. "This is not an easy club to get into." I pulled a bunch of hundred-dollar bills out of my suitcase when I read that—I'd change them into euros at the front desk. All those stolen video projectors were finally paying off. Nothing like a nice tip to get bouncers to see things your way.

Anyway, took us about an hour to spruce ourselves up and get to Cité, and we were there about twelve-fifteen. There was indeed a long line, and these big but elegantly dressed bouncers were patrolling with angry sneers on their faces. The line looked hopeless, so I walked to the front (a little intimidated, I'll admit) and waved over a bouncer.

"English?" I said.

He gave me a look of disgust. "What do you want?" he said.

"I want to get in," I said, and flashed a hundred-euro

note—roughly the value of a hundred-and-thirty bucks. The guy's sneer stayed, but he put out his hand, and in the next instant Erika, Ruben, and I were headed through the ropes and into the front door. Money. Not bad.

Anyway, it was pretty cool inside. Huge, dark, red velvet couches everywhere, booming music. Like a carnival. And beautiful people. Lots of beautiful people. Looked like another great night on the town for one Evan Macalister. But things actually got a little dicey. Had quite an experience really. It's a bit of a digression. That is, doesn't really have to do with Lubchenko. But it was part of my Paris trip. So, worth telling. Here's the story:

So, Erika disappeared onto the dance floor, and in about ten minutes she came back with three other kids around our age, and they all plopped down on the couches that Ruben and I were guarding.

"Meet my new friends," she said, and then we were introduced to Laurent, Sophie, and Delphine. (For the record, and because French names can be confusing, Laurent was a dude and Sophie and Delphine were women.)

Frankly, the guy was too good-looking for my taste. Can't trust people like that. Especially around Erika. The women, though, were also stunning, so I refrained from making a big scene. And they also happened to be really nice. They were all French, but they went to the French-American school, and their English was almost perfect. Apparently, this is a big school in Paris, and all sorts of people go there, although both Sophie and Delphine had American mothers.

Anyway, we all said we were pleased to meet each other, and then Laurent asked what we were doing in Paris.

"Just vacation," I said.

"Spring break?" Delphine asked.

"Spring break," Ruben replied, kind of excited by these women suddenly arriving.

Apparently, however, Sophie and Laurent were going out, as I figured out when they started holding hands. So Sophie was off the table. But Delphine was now definitely available. And Ruben couldn't believe his luck.

Sadly for Ruben, however, she was more into me. Kind of subtle. Hard to tell if you don't know what you're looking at. But she was definitely paying more attention to me. Sad that this kind of thing always happened when I was out with Ruben.

"Do you play American football?" she asked me.

"Actually, I play rugby," I said. "I'm a rugby player. I love rugby."

"Really," she said. "It's such a dangerous sport."

Then Ruben chimed in: "I play American football." I almost burst out laughing but then thought that wouldn't be nice. Still, the image of Ruben playing football was pretty funny. Almost as funny as me playing rugby.

Anyway, the truth is that Erika, Ruben, and I were excited to have company, and for the next hour or so, we all chatted, got up and danced, drank elegant-looking cocktails, and had a great time.

The other good thing was that I think Delphine grooving on me kind of bothered Erika a bit—as far as I could tell, at least.

In fact, this is how I knew that Delphine was at least somewhat interested—Erika was a little protective. She kept glancing over at us, and when she'd catch my eye, she'd scrunch up her nose and leer at me.

And at one point, when Ruben (in an act of inexplicable bravado) grabbed Delphine's hand and pulled her onto the dance floor, Erika quickly got up, sat next to me, leaned over, and said, "Ooh, Evan, knockout French girl kind of into you, huh?"

"Please," I replied. "This kind of thing happens to me all the time. It's really no big deal."

"Uh-huh," Erika said.

"It's true. I'm a heartbreaker. You know that."

"The stud of the Seattle club scene, eh?"

"That's right."

Anyway, all good-natured teasing. Very enjoyable, in fact, since I seemed to be getting into Erika's head. In fact, I was kind of thinking that this might be the night for me to put the world-famous Evan Macalister moves on her. But then something pretty crazy happened. Again, not really something relevent to the whole Lubchenko thing. But still pretty crazy.

So this was a cool club. No question. Very young and hip. But we did find out about it from a guidebook. Didn't really know that much about it in terms of its street rep. And the book did describe it with the phrase *young people run wild*. What that meant, we weren't really sure. But all of a sudden—and really out of nowhere—the lights suddenly shot on, the music ground to a halt, and into the club ran about forty cops. One had a bullhorn and was screaming something I can roughly translate as, "Stay the hell where you are."

Kind of incredible, really. A raid. Incredible. Of course, no one listened to the cop with the bullhorn. No one stayed where they were. There was all sorts of running, panic, mayhem, etc. Ruben, Delphine, Sophie, and Laurent eventually made it back to our table, while other people darted back and forth, yelling, calling out for friends, getting on their cell phones, etc. Pretty crazy.

Laurent just smiled as he sat down next to me and Erika.

"Nothing to worry about," he said. "They've been having problems with ecstasy at Parisian clubs lately. It's been in the news, and the mayor promised to do something about it. So there have been some raids. Especially where young people hang out. A new thing. In my opinion, I don't think they have the right to do this. But apparently there've been rumors that drug dealers have been coming here. The cops won't bother us, though. Might ask us a few questions. But I don't think we look too suspicious."

Of course, what Laurent didn't know is that I'm the most suspicious-looking man that ever lived. People in authority take one look at me, and they call out the armed services, even (or especially) when I'm totally innocent. And this time was no exception. Apparently, this look I have, this talent I have for arousing suspicion, was just as powerful in France as it was in the United States.

In about five minutes a cop came over to where we were sitting, looked us over, asked us a few questions, which Erika and Laurent answered, and then the guy pointed his finger at me and told me, in ridiculous English, to stand up and come with him.

"What's going on?" I quickly asked Laurent.

"I think they want to give you a drug test," he said.

"What?" I yelled. "Can they do that?"

"You can refuse. But then you're looking at lots of official red tape. New rules. You might never leave France. I'll try to talk them out of it. But if you're clean, I say just do it. You don't want to get hung up in the French bureaucracy."

What could I do? Good thing I was so squeaky clean. Still, Laurent tried to intervene. Told the cops that I was an American tourist and that I shouldn't have to go through this kind of thing.

When they asked me (again, in terrible English), "Where are your parents? Can they come down and identify you?" I had to shrug and try to explain that I was just a sixteen-year-old staying on his own at the Ritz with some school chums on a little holiday. Not illegal. But definitely suspicious. In the next second, I was being escorted back to the men's room, where there were a bunch of other dudes going through the same thing. This, of course, is where my years of troublemaking paid off. I was cool as a cucumber. Even when the guy with long white latex gloves followed me into the stall.

"You think I'm scared?" I said as the white-gloved cop

scowled at me. I was pretty sure he didn't understand me, but I also mumbled a bit. "I'm not scared," I continued. "I'm from the United States of America. I hope that means something to you, buddy."

Looking back, I've got to think that this was pretty stupid on my part. Never mouth off to a cop, even if you think up a very funny joke. But again, I don't think this guy understood me. Didn't speak English. All he really wanted was the cup. When he got what he wanted, he gave me a card with a number on it and walked me into another room. Then he walked over to this big machine with a laptop computer connected to it. Some kind of analyzer, I assumed, because in the next minute I saw them dump in my sample.

Now, again, I really had nothing to worry about. Stuff like ecstasy just wasn't the sort of trouble I got into. Way out of my league. I just liked ripping off my dad. Still, that French technology seemed pretty unreliable to me. And judging from the way they drove, who knew how these cops would be at working this machine.

At any rate, at a certain point, they started reading off numbers. I didn't understand what they were saying. Technically, I knew my numbers in French. But once you hear an actual French person saying them, it's hard to understand. The only way I knew I was up is that they read the number about twenty-five times. Eventually, a cop walked over, looked at all our numbers, then started screaming at me.

"I have no idea what you're saying," I said. "I don't understand."

He looked pensive for a moment and then said, "You are innocent. Go now." Then he pointed toward the door. Good news. A relief. But what a joke it all was. Piss in a cup. There's a story about international intrigue to tell people back home.

When I got back into the club, everyone was waiting for me. Apparently, they were making parents come pick up the kids who were sixteen and younger. And as for tourists that didn't have their passports on them (Erika, Ruben, and me), they were going to discuss this matter. They weren't sure what to do. It turned out Laurent, Sophie, and Delphine were sixteen, so someone was going to have to pick them up as well. But they seemed pretty calm.

"Laurent's father is coming to get us," Delphine told me. "He'll be able to take us all home."

Laurent's father arrived in another five minutes. He was some kind of high-level authority in France's Department of Trade. This, at least, is what Delphine told me, and he sure looked the part. Tall, million-dollar suit, fantastic haircut, chiseled jawline. Very imposing.

Anyway, he walked in, talked to Laurent for a few minutes, and then just started screaming at the head cop. I understood nothing, of course, but did hear the words *liberty* and *American* several times. Laurent walked over to me. "He's pretty upset that they gave you a drug test," he said.

"It was no big deal," I replied. "I don't want to make a fuss."

Laurent smiled. "My father can get pretty pissed off in this kind of situation. He works for the government, but he doesn't like it when the police overstep their authority."

I actually started getting nervous at this point. Was thinking we all should have stayed home and laid low. The whole thing had *international incident* written all over it. We had something major to accomplish, and this could really mess it up. I mean, I didn't need anyone asking me any more questions. What the hell was I going to say if this cop decided to push this matter? Granted, maybe an unlikely scenario, but I'm a paranoid man. I was imagining all sorts of news headlines about this—BATTLE OVER CIVIL LIBERTIES IN FRANCE. AMERICAN TEEN AT THE CENTER. That would be quite a thing to have to explain to my dad. Kept hearing him yelling, "You're alone for the first time in your life and you fly off to Paris to do drugs at a discotheque."

And then, for some reason, I thought about that time he'd left me in jail for a night, and again how different he was from Laurent's father, who was there trying to defend his son and his friends. I mean, I'm not against cops doing their jobs. And I wasn't even that mad that they gave me the drug test. Maybe there really was a problem with ecstasy at clubs in Paris. Who knows? And I'll tell you another thing: I hate it when parents always think their kids are so innocent. Nothing worse than a clueless parent who thinks his darling children can do no wrong and is always hiring lawyers and yelling at cops to protect their sorry asses. I really do hate that. Still, there's a balance. And my father was way on the other end of the spectrum. Always assume Evan is guilty—that was his policy. It was again clear to me that I did not have a father who would ever go to bat for me like this. Very depressing.

Anyway, after about ten minutes of screaming, it was time to go. Laurent's father had apparently made sure they'd let the young and innocent American tourists leave. As we were headed out, I was then introduced to Laurent's father, and I thanked him for getting us out of trouble. He shook my hand, apologized with great sincerity, and asked us if we had a way to get home.

"I would drive you," he said, "but I'm afraid my car will already be full with these three."

"A cab's easiest for us anyway," I said.

Then, after a few brief goodbyes, we jumped in a cab and were headed back to the Ritz.

The truth was, though, that we were pretty riled up. Not sleepy at all. Hungry. I was, at least, although I figured it was the same for everyone when Ruben suddenly suggested that we get food at an all-night café called Le Biarritz that was near the hotel. "I can't sleep right now," Ruben said. "That was crazy. That was totally crazy. What if I had to call my parents in Seattle?"

I laughed, but when I looked over at Ruben, I could see that he was really shaken up. "That was really close, Evan," Ruben continued. "I hate having to explain myself to cops in situations like that."

"Ruben," I said, "nothing bad happened. We're in good shape."

Ruben paused, then said with a bit more force, "Coming to Paris was the worst idea you've ever had, Evan. I can't believe we're doing this."

"We're fine, Ruben," I said, although I was having my own doubts. And I kind of felt bad. Ruben was always in a state of panic, but he seemed especially freaked out now. I mean, maybe I shouldn't have always dragged Ruben along with my stupid ideas. Very troubling.

Finally I just said, "We need food. Food's a good idea." It was six in the morning at this point (actually about when clubs in Paris normally close), and I think we all needed to decompress over steaks and french fries.

31

S o steaks at Le Biarritz. And lots of chatter. The place was jam-packed. Six o'clock really is when the club scene ends, and everyone and his tarted-up cousin seemed to be looking for food to help them calm down from an exciting night of dancing.

Ruben was still kind of freaked out. Kind of depressed too. Wasn't good. But the food helped. A big steak covered in *sauce au poivre* (pepper sauce—one of the few French phrases I actually know) kind of did the trick for him. In fact, we all quickly shut up when the food came. I tried to talk. I asked Ruben if he was enjoying his food. But he just looked up at me and said, "I don't want to talk. No talking right now."

Suited me.

Anyway, by seven-thirty in the morning we were staggering into the Ritz, feeling like rock star partyers as we passed the doormen, but knowing full well we almost got in big trouble that night. And then the elevator. And then the hallway. And then bed. We had things to do the next day—we knew that. But we were all so excited about bed that we didn't say anything about it. Just went to sleep.

And it was great, the sleeping. Really great. The thing is that

I don't think anyone thought it would go on for so long. And when Ruben banged on my door at five the next evening (still only 8 a.m. Seattle time), I was wondering what had happened and where I was and why I wasn't already awake and tracking down Lubchenko.

"Get up, Evan," Ruben was screaming as I was trying to open my eyes. "It's already night again. Get up."

"All right, all right," I yelled, finally realizing that we had all been asleep for most of the day. I got up to let Ruben in, but when I opened the door, he was across the hall, in his boxers, banging on Erika's door. "Get up," he screamed. "Time to get going."

Anyway, in about five minutes, we were all sitting on my bed, talking about what we should do. We had basically wasted a day. We were supposed to go to Lubchenko Auto but had missed that. And it was really too late to head out now.

"I feel like such an idiot," Ruben said. "Out all night drinking. Sleeping all day. We've wasted valuable time."

"We're fine, Ruben," I said. "We'll go to the garage tomorrow. We're still moving forward."

"We should see if there are any messages for us," Erika said.

This was a good point. Maybe Lubchenko had called and the Champlan trip was moot. I quickly jumped up, ran to the elevator, and headed to the lobby.

"Hello, Mr. Macalister," Henri said as I arrived.

"Hi, Henri," I replied. "Just wanted to see if there were any messages for me."

He smiled, turned, and disappeared into a back room. In another minute, he returned and said, "I'm afraid not. Were you expecting something?"

"Kind of," I said. "But no big deal." Then I turned and headed back to my room.

"No luck," I said as I got back. "What now?"

Ruben groaned, but he seemed calmer by this point. Still, he did find the strength to make one pessimistic remark: "We're all going to jail," he said.

"Uh, you guys are going to jail," Erika said. "I'm not going to jail. I haven't done anything wrong."

"I'm very sorry," Ruben said. "Correction: Evan and I are going to jail."

"Thank you," Erika said.

Anyway, after talking for a few more minutes, we decided to head back to Tien-Fu to continue staking out Café Saint-Beauvais. It wasn't much of a plan. But what else did we have to do? We could sit by the front desk, hoping Lubchenko got in touch with us. But that was hardly like doing much.

Anyway, back to Tien-Fu. Eight million more dumplings and egg rolls. Groggy and uninteresting conversation. Useless vigilance of Café Saint-Beauvais (nothing odd or strange seemed to be happening; no suspicious characters). And by eleven, we were headed back to the Ritz.

"We've only been awake for six hours and now we're going back to bed," I said. Seemed strange. But we really were exhausted. Funny how drinking cocktails all night and then sleeping all day can leave you so fatigued. Anyway, what else did we have to do? The best thing for us was to get a good night's sleep so we'd be fresh the next day.

"Any messages, Henri?" I asked as we entered the lobby of the Ritz.

"I've been keeping a lookout for you, Mr. Macalister," Henri said. "But I'm afraid nothing has come in."

Somehow I wasn't surprised.

So, next morning. The Parisian suburb of Champlan. The trip only took about forty minutes. First we jumped on the subway and then on the commuter rail that headed out of the city. It was early by my standards but still after rush hour—about 10 a.m. All in all, an easy trip.

We were using a map we'd picked up in a bookstore not far from the hotel, and the garage was fairly easy to find. Only about a ten-minute walk from the train station. And it was a pleasant walk. Lots of pleasant sights. It was like we were real live tourists. Still, we had a lot on our minds. I did, at least. In the harsh, clear light of the morning, I kind of started regretting the nights of clubbing, the day spent in bed, and my less-than-serious attitude in general. The stakes were really high. They didn't get any higher. For my father and for me. And I wasn't exactly rising to the occasion, as they say. Maybe I really was the wastrel my father thought I was. Hopefully we could turn something up that morning, and I wouldn't feel like I was just spinning my wheels.

Anyway, as we approached the garage (me still feeling slightly out of sorts), we kind of reverted to the plan we used at the Saint-Beauvais. That is, we told Erika to do the talking.

"But don't mess it up," I said.

"If you had ever done any French homework, Evan, you could probably handle this yourself," she said.

"Just don't mess it up," I said again, but kind of smiled. Just a little harmless teasing to keep us loose.

The garage looked like it was a hundred years old and hadn't been painted once in all that time. It might have been white once. That's what it looked like. By this point, though, it was just a kind of gray, chipped stucco supported by old wooden beams. There were also a bunch of beat-up cars out front, which didn't add much to the place's appearance. Still, two big garage doors were open and there were guys in there working on cars, so they seemed to be doing some kind of business. And there was also a pretty big sign above the door. It said LUBCHENKO AUTO, so we were clearly at the right place.

When we walked into the little office at the side of the shop, we were met by an old woman standing behind the counter, looking very suspiciously at us. Seemed like she was about to reach for a shotgun, in fact. And she didn't look any friendlier as we approached the counter. Despite the deep wrinkles in her face and her very gray hair, she had clear, penetrating, steely eyes, and she was paying close attention to us.

"Yes?" she said in a crisp, clear voice. (Again, a translation from the French.)

"Hello," Erika replied, kind of stammering. "We were wondering if you could help us. We're looking for someone. Is there a Mr. Lubchenko here?" Erika paused. "Or a Ms. Lubchenko?"

It was a good question. Maybe this woman was the Lubchenko that had been corresponding with Belachek. Would be a shock. But not impossible.

"No," she said. "No Lubchenko." Her French didn't seem so good—she spoke with something that sounded like a Russian accent. (Like lots of American cities, Paris is full of travelers and immigrants, so it was no surprise that she sounded Russian, especially in a place called Lubchenko Auto.) The woman seemed to have more to say than, "No Lubchenko," however. She hesitated a bit and then said, "English? English?"

"Yes," we all replied, kind of relieved, and in the next second we were talking to her in our mother tongue.

Now, I have to say that her English wasn't that good either, but what she had to say wasn't that complicated. There was a man named Lubchenko, she said. But he was dead. "Dead. Gone. Dead. Dead," she said.

Apparently, he had been dead for a few months and when we asked how he died, the woman just said, "Sick. Very sick. Old and sick. Sick for years. Old man." Then she pointed to a picture of an old, kind of stooped man standing in front of the garage, right under the Lubchenko sign. "That's him. Old there. Ten years ago."

"Did he have any family?" Ruben asked. "Is there another Lubchenko?"

"No. No family. Only workers here." She pointed to the mechanics walking around the shop. "And me. I am girlfriend. But I'm no Lubchenko. Lubchenko not my name. I'm just girlfriend." At this point she flashed us a big grin that revealed she was missing several teeth. Somewhat shocking, really. I guess old people have boyfriends and girlfriends too. But this woman was not exactly the girlfriend you'd imagine a high-end spy having. I would have expected someone a bit more like Halle Berry. Maybe even Britney Spears. This woman just didn't seem to be a likely candidate. And that made *her* Lubchenko less likely to be *our* Lubchenko.

Anyway, we were fumbling for the next question when she asked us what we were looking for.

"What you want with him?" she said. "Why you looking for him?" She was still kind of smiling, but she also looked a bit apprehensive.

"It's not important," I said. "I don't think it's the Lubchenko we're looking for. Are you sure there's not another Lubchenko?"

The woman looked like she was trying hard to think, then she said, "No. Only one Lubchenko. All alone. Except for me." She smiled again. She looked like she might even start laughing. And then the smile suddenly disappeared. In fact, she looked like she was a little sad, and she said, "He was my boyfriend, and now I'm all alone too."

Kind of heavy. Suddenly kind of touching. I think we all wanted to go behind the counter and hug her. But that really might have freaked her out.

Anyway, it was pretty clear to me that the old man on the wall wasn't the Lubchenko we were looking for. Or it was at least clear that this woman was telling us everything that she knew. Again, I think we had all vaguely hoped that some young, strapping man would walk out of the back room and say, "I'm Lubchenko, I am a great international spy, and I've been expecting you." Sadly, no such luck.

So we smiled, thanked the woman several times, and then left.

The trip back was kind of depressing. Kind of like how we felt after our visit to Saint-Beauvais, although the café still seemed to hold some promise. The garage, on the other hand, seemed totally useless. It seemed that way. Ruben, however, had a different take on it, which he shared with us on the train ride home.

"You know," he said, tapping his fingers on the armrest and looking around nervously, "I hate to be paranoid. But I'm really thinking that walking into these places and announcing we're looking for some shady character named Lubchenko might not be such a good idea. We think he's a friend. But we don't really know much about him. I mean, we keep talking about how we'll just turn over everything to the FBI if we don't turn anything up. But what if Lubchenko and company don't actually want us to do that? We're walking around Paris, telling all sorts of people that we're here and we know some secret stuff and that we're trying to capture a killer. All pretty stupid, if you ask me. I mean, who knows what's going on at Lubchenko Auto? Some ninety-year-old woman says her boyfriend is dead, but who knows what's really going on? Maybe she's on the phone right now telling the Russian mafia about us. The guy from Café Saint-Beauvais too. It won't take more than a few phone calls to figure out that the son of the guy who's been framed for Belachek's murder is now in Paris sticking his nose into other people's business. I mean, we more or less even told that to the Saint-Beauvais guy." By the time he got to this point, Ruben's voice had gotten higher, and he was looking at Erika and me with a kind of frantic expression. But it was hard to know what to say. He was making good points. It was the same old dilemma. Were we really saving our asses, or were we digging ourselves in deeper? I will admit that I have a tendency to dig deeper in these situations. But at this point, it just seemed best to move forward.

"We'll be careful," I said. "I think we're doing the right thing. But we should be careful."

Ruben gave me kind of a hesitant look. "We could just head to the U.S. Embassy tonight and turn ourselves in."

It was an option. But I thought about what it would be like to get busted for stealing from MRI and (much worse at this point) withholding evidence on a murder case. Pretty rough. Would pretty much be the end of my life. Seemed like we had to stick to the plan.

"We'll be fine," I said. "We're going to be fine. We need to see this through, though."

Ruben looked at me, still kind of worried, and then looked out the window. He still appeared kind of despondent. Finally he said, "Maybe there'll be a message from Lubchenko at the Ritz."

Good to hear him say something that was at least a bit hopeful.

But after the train arrived in Paris and we walked back to the hotel, we discovered that there was not, in fact, a message waiting for us. Ruben didn't really react. We all just slowly walked to the elevator and headed up to our rooms.

It was only early afternoon when we got back from Champlan, so after showers and asking again for messages at the Ritz's front desk, we headed back to Tien-Fu to eat more shrimp toast and continue our stakeout of Café Saint-Beauvais.

33

"I've never had so much Chinese food in my life," Ruben said as he looked over the plates and plates of dumplings and egg rolls that were in front of us.

"Well, this is what they say to do when you come to Paris," I replied. "Spend hours in Chinese restaurants."

Erika smiled and poked me in the ribs. "Always a wise guy," she said.

We stayed there for most of the afternoon and early evening. It really was kind of pointless. We didn't recognize anyone and didn't see anything unusual. The only reason we were doing it was because we couldn't think of anything else to do.

Anyway, I'd report more if I could, but nothing happened. So we kind of packed it in early. Surveillance was yielding nothing. We were bored. Frustrated. We started thinking that Lubchenko might have sent us a message—we were dreaming—and we wanted to check in again at the Ritz. And there's only so much Chinese food you can see and smell in one day.

The one thing we had to decide was what to do that night. Another night of clubbing?

"Not me," Ruben said as we were crossing a large pedestrian bridge that spanned the Seine. "I can't take another night out. Or I can't take another sluggish, hung-over day."

I was considering saying the same thing, but Erika jumped in first. "Well, I want to go out," she said. "And I know you do, too, Evan."

Funny how a man can go from thoughts of frustration and doom to thoughts of happy optimism in a single second.

"Of course," I said. "I wouldn't let you go out in this dangerous city alone."

"Well, you guys have fun," Ruben said, now looking at me out of the corner of his eye. "But count me out. Someone has to be chipper for tomorrow. We've got to be alert as we scarf down kung pao chicken."

"Good point," I said. "You're in charge of that. Make sure you're prepared."

Anyway, after getting back to the hotel and checking for messages (for the millionth time), we headed to our rooms. Quick nap. Lounging around. Shower. And then careful physical grooming. Wanted to look my best. Then, at about eight-thirty, I heard a knock on my door. "Let's go, Macalister," Erika yelled.

"All right," I replied. I opened the door, let her get a good long look at me, and said, "Let's go, honey." And off we went.

34

E rika and I hadn't actually picked a place to go, so we decided to ask Henri at the front desk for a recommendation.

"What are you looking for?" Henri said.

"Fun," Erika said. "We want to have fun. Noisy, lots of people, a dance floor, live music."

Henri thought for a moment, then recommended a place called La Vanoise. "It's quite unusual for Paris," he said. "It serves food you might find in the French Alps. Has a country theme. Very loud. And always live music with dancing. Something like polka dancing. If you like polka dancing."

My first thought was to say, "Yeah, right," but Erika quickly started jumping up and down.

"Yes, yes, yes, yes. We're going polka dancing."

"It's not technically polka dancing," Henri said. "But it's close. It's country dancing. Like square dancing, maybe, in the United States."

"Yes, yes, yes," Erika said again.

I still wasn't sure. I was still kind of in the mood for some kind of snobby white-dinner-jacket place. But once Erika starts jumping up and down, it's hard to talk her out of something.

"Looks like you have no choice, Mr. Macalister," Henri said.

"Looks like it," I replied.

The restaurant was north of the Ritz, in an area near this huge church called the Sacré Coeur—or sacred heart. Worth seeing—big, white, bulbous thing that looks like several enormous and upside-down turnips. Very holy. Very inspiring.

Anyway, the cab didn't take too long, and in no time Erika and I were heading through the doors of La Vanoise. As we walked in, we definitely heard music, but it was kind of muffled and we couldn't see where it was coming from. In fact, everything seemed kind of tame and simple. Nice decor. Lots of wooden beams and old skis and pictures of cows—French Alp stuff. Lots of people having dinner. But kind of quiet.

"We heard there was dancing here," Erika said when the maitre d' arrived.

"Of course," he said. "There is the best dancing in the world here. But you have to go downstairs."

The man escorted us to an enormous stone staircase, and as we headed down, the music got louder and louder. Was actually kind of a cool feeling, descending into the depths of this old building. The staircase was solid stone and looked like it was built five hundred years ago. Probably was.

By the time we arrived at the bottom of the stairs, we realized that this was where the action was. There were plenty of people eating dinner—which was good because I was hungry—but there was another huge crowd on the dance floor, all jumping around while this five-piece band (an accordion, a drum set, two unidentifiable string instruments, and one unidentifiable horn) played this carnival-type music. Sounded like polka to me. But what do I know?

"This is great," Erika yelled. "This is exactly what I wanted."

Good that she was so excited, but I have to say that I was pretty into it too. We were in what looked like an enormous stone wine cellar, lit almost entirely by candles and filled with deliriously happy people scooping melted cheese into their mouths. My kind of place.

We sat down quickly and looked over the menus.

"I think we have to go with the fondue," I said. It seemed to be almost the only thing on the menu. There was a small paragraph explaining that French Alpine people spend almost every waking moment eating melted cheese. Seemed a reasonable way to live your life to me.

Whatever. Melted cheese, wine, dancing, happy people. You get the picture. Now to the more important part.

Erika and I had a great dinner. And then we started dancing. Lots of fun. There were plenty of top-notch dancers out there on the dance floor. But there were also freaks like us who had no idea what they were doing. And I've got to say it was a pretty good time. We danced almost every dance after we finished eating, and in a form of body art that doesn't actually require much contact, she was certainly hanging on me. I don't know. It was something.

But for some unknown reason, I started having these feelings of guilt. I am not a mature man. I am not a man of mature emotions. Still, it occurred to me that maybe there was something wrong with harboring this crush for as long as I had. Crushes aren't exactly anyone's fault. But this was one of my closest friends, and I had been turning every interaction into some opportunity to score.

Still, scoring was pretty appealing. Pretty appealing. I like scoring. Yep. So, a real dilemma, especially because it required action. This is not the kind of ethical problem that's best discussed in a classroom. If you choose a certain direction, you've got to come up with the moves. Got to have the moves.

And as usual, I did not. I did not have the moves. She was clinging to me. We were in the midst of a huge crowd of happy, dancing people. And we were even a little drunk. But I couldn't do it. I just couldn't bring myself to try to kiss her. And so we danced, had a great time, tired ourselves out, and at about 2 a.m., once we were completely exhausted, we left La Vanoise, me no further with Erika than I'd ever been and still feeling remorse over constantly dealing with this idiotic crush.

And I think that's what kind of got to me. We hailed a cab. Erika said, "That was so much fun, Evan, thank you so much." And I just sat there thinking, *Macalister, you're a complete idiot. Will you do something about this?*

But nothing. I was capable of nothing. And as we walked in the front door of the Ritz, and got onto the elevator, and stepped onto our hall, I was thinking that I'd never have another opportunity like this in my life. We were in the middle of the most beautiful city in the world. We were staying at that city's most beautiful hotel. We were engaged in highly dangerous international spy stuff. And we had just spent the night drinking and dancing. What more does a man need?

I could only conclude that my father had been right all these years—I was an imbecile and deserved nothing but shame and ridicule. And then we were at our doors. And it was time to say good night.

"That was so great, Evan," Erika said, turning to me. And then she stood up on her toes to give me a hug before entering her room. But then she pulled back slightly, and as she did, our cheeks grazed, and in the next second (shockingly) we were kissing. Only for a second. A couple of seconds, maybe. Maybe about ten seconds. But by the time I was aware of what was happening, she had pulled back and we were suddenly just kind of staring at each other. I can't say that the kiss was my fault. I really don't think it was. But Erika definitely looked a little freaked out.

"I'm sorry," I said. "I'm sorry."

Erika paused for a second, then reached behind her and opened the door to her room. Then she leaned backward, said, "Good night," and disappeared into her room.

As I stood there in the hallway, I tried to figure out what had just happened. I almost knocked on Erika's door so we could have a long discussion about it. I do such stupid things from time to time. But finally I decided we'd talk later.

It just wasn't what I had imagined such a thing would be

like. I mean, I wasn't even thinking I'd do anything, and then we were kissing, and then I apologized, and then she ran into her room. That was it? That was the big move? All very troubling. The best thing I could come up with was to head to my room and get into bed. Seemed to be my solution for everything these days. Still, even bed didn't help that much. The fact was that, for whatever reason, we kissed, and Erika reacted by running away. Very depressing.

35

My first thoughts the next morning were of the kiss. Strange, given all that was going on. Still, these thoughts didn't last long. Or they led to another set of thoughts. They led to a pretty central fact that was now staring me in the face: It was our last day in Paris and we had achieved absolutely nothing. We had spent a lot of money, eaten a lot of dumplings, chilled in several groovy clubs, but as far as saving my ass went, nada. We hadn't found anyone named Lubchenko. We had captured no killers. We had uncovered no key piece of evidence. It suddenly looked like it was over for me, like I was going to have to go to the FBI with the laptop.

Anyway, in about half an hour, we were dressed and standing in the hall. Erika and I kind of gave each other sheepish looks. But nothing more than that. We had to stay on task.

"Tien-Fu?" I said.

"Tien-Fu," Ruben replied.

We went downstairs, asked Henri for messages—there were none—and then we were off.

I have to say that it did kind of feel hopeless—this stakeout. A waste of time. But we couldn't figure out a better way to waste our time, so that's what we did.

So, it was a little after ten in the morning when we arrived at Tien-Fu, and it was totally empty. But the front doors were open, and no one turned us away from the table, so we began the day with a late breakfast of fried rice and wonton soup. Have to say, not bad food to begin the day with. We also talked about possible evasive action we could take. But what could we do?

"Maybe we should go back to Café Saint-Beauvais and ask for Lubchenko again," Erika suggested. We all looked out the window toward the café for a moment and thought about this.

"If the guy told us no once, he's probably not going to change his mind," Ruben said.

"Maybe Lubchenko changed his mind and wants to meet us now," Erika said.

"Then he would have contacted us at the Ritz," I said.

"Well, what do we have to lose by asking again?" Erika asked.

"Lubchenko could get agitated and send some goons over here and pop us," Ruben replied.

"No one's going to 'pop' us," I said. There was a brief pause, and then I sighed. Suddenly felt pretty lame. "Maybe the guy doesn't even know Lubchenko. Probably the case. This was probably all just a wild-goose chase. Four thin e-mails led us here. Not much. And frankly, we don't actually know what we're doing."

"This is very true," Ruben said.

Again, a pause. Suddenly things felt even more hopeless, more depressing.

And then, in a sudden, strange, and terrible moment, things fell into place. Or they became more confused. We finally realized that we were on to something.

As I cast my gaze down to the street, I saw something that honestly made my heart stop. At first I thought I had it wrong. But as the man came closer, I realized it was who I thought it was. Still, I couldn't believe it. It was Rick Colburn. He was walking from the other direction, from beyond the Saint-Beauvais. He was moving quickly, keeping his eyes straight ahead of him and looking just as cold as he always did.

I was so startled, I barely knew what to say. Finally I gasped, "Oh my God." Ruben and Erika saw that I spotted something and quickly turned around to look out the window. And just about at that moment, Colburn turned and went into the Saint-Beauvais.

"What?" Ruben said. "What did you see?"

I was so shocked, I almost couldn't speak. Finally I said, "Rick Colburn. I saw Rick Colburn. He just went into the Saint-Beauvais."

And then there was a very heavy and chilling silence.

"We're dead," Ruben finally said.

I looked at Ruben and for the first time couldn't bring myself to contradict him. Funny how much can change in a matter of a minute. What was theoretical and speculative had now just become completely real. Café Saint-Beauvais was now undoubtedly part of all this, and Colburn was definitely involved. Kind of stunning to see it all laid out like that.

L ooking back, I suppose we should have been a little more prepared for such sur-  prises. We had come to Paris without much of an idea of what we'd find, so it's hard to say why we should have been so shocked to see Colburn. But we were. And it was totally baffling. Did not know what to think.

We decided to stay put for the next stretch—to watch the Saint-Beauvais until Colburn came out again. But this wasn't a quick visit. And for the next half hour, we saw absolutely noth-ing. Unfortunately, from Tien-Fu we didn't have a great view inside the restaurant. That is, Colburn was in a part of the café we couldn't see. It was unfortunate, especially because it would have really helped us out to have seen who he was talking to.

"We've got to get a better look," Erika said.

After discussing it a little, we decided to send Ruben down to try to catch a glimpse inside the Saint-Beauvais. From street level, he'd be able to see what Colburn was up to. But it was risky, and Ruben wasn't too excited about the task.

"I don't want to. I don't want to," he said about eighteen times.

But it had to be Ruben. Colburn obviously knew me, and

36

he'd met Erica. And the owner was more likely to recognize Erika than Ruben since she was the one who'd talked to him.

"It's got to be you," I said. "But we'll be right here. Don't go in. If someone jumps you, we'll call the cops." I pointed to a phone that hung from the wall.

Ruben gritted his teeth and then slowly stood up. He really looked scared. This wasn't his normal paranoid act. He really looked like he was going to lose it.

"We'll be right here," Erika said. "You'll be fine."

"I wish people would stop telling me that. It's never, ever true." Then Ruben forced a weak smile and headed for the stairs, and in a few seconds Erika and I saw him walk onto the street.

Ruben walked slowly. He was trying to be cool. But even from the second floor, I could see he was kind of shaking. Fortunately, there were a couple of cars and a minivan parked on that side of the street, so he could get a good look without being seen. He stood there for about five minutes, barely moving. It looked like he was searching every corner of the café. Then he suddenly turned, looked up at us, and shrugged. In the next instant, he was on his way back up. And when he arrived, all he could say was, "He wasn't in there."

"Are you sure?" I said.

"I got a good look at the whole café. I didn't see him."

My first thought was that he might have ducked out the back. Then Erika suggested the more likely possibility: "I bet he's in the back office or in a back room. And if that's true, it means that he definitely knows the owner. If there is a guy named Lubchenko hiding out there, he's got to be in touch with him."

Kind of chilling. Still, we weren't sure. And we didn't exactly know what to do. The best thing we could do was wait. We wanted to see Colburn again. "Maybe Colburn will leave with someone," I said.

It was another half hour before Colburn showed his face again. He looked the same. Eyes forward. Cold, deliberate expression. He was still alone, though. He paused slightly as he left the door and then turned and headed back in the direction he had come. We watched the door for another minute, but no one else came out. I looked at Erika and Ruben, and then they looked back at me.

"What now?" I said.

At this point, Ruben suddenly turned very pale. "You know," he said, his voice now kind of strained, "I hate to be such a downer all the time, and I hate to even bring this up, but we left our address with the Saint-Beauvais owner. If they're in with Colburn, that probably means he knows we're on to him. It means he knows we're here and where we're staying. And since this is probably the guy who killed Belachek, I can't imagine that he'd have much of a problem icing us."

Again, an instant of silence. Now we were all extremely pale.

"We've got to get out of the Ritz," I said. And with that, we jumped up, paid our bill, and headed back to the hotel.

37

S o here was the plan. We came up with it on the way back. We decided it probably wasn't a good idea to make a big show of leaving the hotel. If we weren't going to stay the night at the Ritz, the best thing we could do was pretend we were there. That way, if Colburn decided to cut our throats during the night, he'd be in the wrong spot. But we did need our plane tickets and passports and a few other things. As for our clothes and suitcases, we were just going to leave them behind. This didn't seem to bother anyone, though. We were kind of just focusing on the matter at hand. "We're so dead," Ruben screamed. "We're so dead. I can't believe we're doing this. We should just go to the police now."

"An option," I replied. "Definitely an option. But let's keep our cool for just a little while longer. We're in this far. Let's not rush into anything."

Still, it really did seem like the game was now over. I kept thinking about my father screaming at me once we came clean, and it made me sick. Made me almost as sick as the idea of Colburn putting a bullet in my head.

But we had to stay focused. Surviving seemed to be the priority at this point. It was just all so confusing. The place we thought was "friendly" was being visited by a murderer. The murderer was in town. He probably knew where we were staying. And he probably knew we were after him. This was as life-and-death as it gets.

My mind raced through all the various possibilities and scenarios, and as we approached the Ritz, I stopped everyone to bring up one final concern.

"Colburn could be on his way up to our rooms right now," I said. "Erika, give me your key. We'll get your ticket and passport for you. You wait in the lobby. If we're not down in ten minutes, start screaming."

"Okay," she said. "Makes sense."

We all took a deep breath and walked past the bellhop and through the front entrance of the Ritz. Erika stopped, and Ruben and I walked swiftly to the elevator.

It took us exactly eight minutes to make it up to the rooms and back. We ran around like crazy people, only taking exactly what we needed, which was basically nothing. Everything else was left behind. Kind of tough. Again, was especially unhappy about leaving behind my expensive new suitcase and my excellent suit. But this was an emergency. Having a nice suitcase doesn't mean much if you're dead. There's some wisdom for you.

Anyway, we were back in the lobby in eight minutes, and Erika looked relieved when she saw us. I have to say that I felt pretty relieved seeing her too. But just as we reunited and turned toward the door, I heard a voice call out my name from behind us. I turned quickly, ready to start screaming myself. But it was just Henri from behind the front desk.

"Excuse me, please," he said. "Mr. Macalister. I have good news. A message finally came for you."

I really almost didn't answer.

"I have a message for you, Mr. Macalister," he said again.

"A message?"

"It was just delivered."

I slowly walked toward the counter. Strange how details become so vivid when you're freaked out, but I was suddenly mesmerized by the three chandeliers that hung over the front desk. There must have been ten thousand pieces of crystal hanging above Henri's head. For some reason, it was just such a stunning image to me, but in the next instant, I was back to reality. I took the note from Henri's hand, thanked him, and then turned back to look at Ruben and Erika. They looked as freaked out as I did as I walked back to them.

"Let's sit down for a minute," I said. "We're safe enough here with all these people."

We sat down on a big red velvet couch. I was in the center and we were all looking down at the note. It had my name written on the front, in what was probably the most perfect, official-style handwriting I had ever seen. The paper was pretty thick—cream-colored and definitely very expensive. I paused for another instant and then opened it. The note was short. This is what it said:

> *Dear Mr. Macalister:*
>
> *We have much to discuss. Please come to Café Saint-Beauvais tonight at 9 p.m. I assure you that you will be quite safe.*
>
> —Lubchenko

I t almost seemed like a joke. And if it wasn't a joke, it definitely seemed like a trap.

38

"He can't be serious," Ruben said. "Why now? This is a setup. Now that Colburn's here, we'll definitely get killed. Shot in the face. Strangled. You name it."

This was a good point. It was exactly what I was thinking. Still, we had some time to consider our options. It was now about 1 p.m. At this point, the main thing was to get out of the Ritz.

"Let's find somewhere else to go," I said.

We quickly stood up and headed out the door.

I told Ruben and Erica that I had an idea about where we should go. The Ritz isn't far from another high-end hotel called the Crillon, which I had considered staying at before we came. I wasn't really in the mood for luxury at that moment. But I also didn't want to spend the next bunch of hours looking for a safe and secure spot. I was sure that the Crillon would be very busy and that there'd be lots of staff running around. Colburn probably wouldn't find us there, but if I did, say, discover him hiding in my shower, it was likely that someone could come to my rescue if I started screaming.

We walked for about half an hour, first circling through several streets and then walking through a big park. We wanted to make sure we weren't being followed. After we were sure we were alone, we doubled back to the Crillon and booked a room.

Now, booking a room for the same night you plan to stay is pretty hard in Paris. The city is the number-one tourist destination in the world. Very busy. In fact, almost all of the Crillon's rooms were full. All that was left were three very expensive suites, which had several rooms attached to each other.

"There's really nothing else?" I asked.

"I'm sorry, sir," the man said. "But at such late notice, this is all we can do."

Ruben jumped in here. "Are you insane? Just get the room. What's the point of worrying about money now?"

The man kind of looked at us with a puzzled expression. But what could he say about it?

"All right," I said. "Give us one of the suites."

I really did hate to do it, though, given the fact that there was no way we were going to enjoy it. But Ruben was right. What choice did we have? Just to give you a sense of where we were, though, the price tag was four thousand dollars. For one night. Still, what were we going to do?

As he ran my credit card through the machine, the guy at the desk continued to look at us like it was a bit strange that three kids were dropping that much money at a hotel. But the credit card worked, and I had ID, so he couldn't do much. I wasn't happy that we drew that kind of attention to ourselves. But it was too late at that point. In the next instant, we were on the elevator and headed to the suite.

So, briefly, this suite was absolutely incredible. Two bedrooms. A huge living room with a bar and a fireplace. A view of the river and the Eiffel Tower. Everything. Really astounding. But it was a sign of how focused I was that I barely noticed it at the time. I made a few remarks. Said that it was a shame we couldn't have more fun there that night. But my instinct was not to crack open a beer and start to party. We needed to talk this over. We quickly walked into the suite's living room, sat down on these million-dollar couches, flipped on the gas fireplace, and begin discussing our situation.

Actually, first, we watched Ruben have a little bit of a freak-out.

"I just want to make one point," he said. "We're so dead. We're so dead. We're so dead. We've got to go to the police right now. It's over. I'm not doing this anymore. It's not worth it. I don't want to go to Harvard now. I just want to go home and know all the bad guys are in jail."

"You're going to be the bad guy in jail if we confess now," I said.

"I'm not a bad guy. I'm a good guy. I wouldn't hurt anyone. I want to make the world a better place."

"You're very noble," Erika said.

"Look," I said, "I'm not against packing this whole thing in.

Maybe it is time to cut our losses. I'm not sure I'm too psyched about walking into a trap that Colburn's involved with. But let's think this through."

"You're not really thinking we should meet him," Ruben said. "I mean, you can't possibly be thinking that."

"Look, it's still possible we can trust Lubchenko," I replied. "He was clearly working with Belachek. But he's also clearly got inside information—at least that's what it seems like from the e-mails. He could be a friend and still have a meeting with Colburn. I mean, he must be an inside guy if he knows so much. Anyway, we'll make sure Lubchenko can't do anything to us. We'll take precautions."

"Like what?" Ruben said. "You're crazy. These are killers we're dealing with. And let me just say that I'm not doing anything stupid. Not anymore. You've dragged me down too far, Evan. You're ruining my life."

I might have actually taken offense at this, but Ruben said something along these lines almost every day. Anyway, I figured Ruben was going to be comfortable with at least his part of my plan.

"All we need to do is leave someone behind again," I continued. "We'll just tell Lubchenko that we've got someone waiting for us and that if we don't get back in touch in a set amount of time, that person will call the French police. And Ruben, given all your blubbering, I think we can all agree that you should be the one to stay behind. Also, Erika, we'll need your French."

There was a pause, and then Ruben started up again.

"I think this is really, really stupid. We're not just stealing office printers here, Evan. These are serious dudes. They've already killed one person. And I can't imagine they'd be afraid to do it again."

Erika looked pensive. She was probably the most thoughtful and reasonable one of us all, but she was keeping her mouth shut. I think she was just weighing the options. I don't think she had come down on one side or the other yet.

Finally I said, "Look, Ruben, you're making good points. They all make sense. But we've come pretty far. I think we should see it through. Lubchenko could still be a friend. And if not, we have insurance waiting for us back here at the hotel. He's not going to do anything to us if he knows you're here ready to make a phone call."

There was now a longer pause.

Finally Ruben said, "I definitely get to be the person who stays behind?"

Erika groaned. "Yes, Ruben," she said. "You get to stay behind. How did you end up being such a loser?"

"It's my mother's fault," Ruben said. "She's always spoiled me."

This was true.

There was another pause. And then I said, "So we're going ahead?"

Now Ruben groaned. But he didn't say no. So that was it. It was settled.

We spent the rest of the afternoon hiding out in the suite at the Crillon. We had room service bring us an early dinner, although none of us had much of an appetite. We had huge plates of food and were looking out at the Eiffel Tower as we ate, but none of us did more than pick at our dinners.

As it got closer to the time Erika and I would have to leave, we went over the plan several times, although there wasn't too much to remember. We thought about planting Ruben in one of the hotel's restaurants. None of us liked the idea of him being alone in the suite. But we were on a high floor, and the door had three locks and was pretty thick, so he'd probably be safe enough.

"Anyway," Erika pointed out, "if Colburn has a high-powered rifle, you sitting out in an open restaurant isn't a very good idea."

"Thanks," Ruben said, frowning. "I'll stay away from the windows, too."

The other issue was timing. We figured that it would take about a half hour. But we could be wrong about this. Who knew what Lubchenko was going to do with us? We finally decided on an hour and a half. The meeting was at nine. If Ruben didn't hear from us by ten-thirty, then he was to call the police at ten thirty-one. We had the hotel's phone number, so if we couldn't make it back in time, we could also call.

And we also came up with an emergency plan if, say, Lubchenko had a gun to our head and made us call. "If I call and say, 'Everything's A-OK,'" I said, "that means Lubchenko is forcing me to make the call and we're in trouble. So, 'A-OK' is code. It means call the police. Got it?"

"Got it," Ruben said. Ruben at this point, by the way, was starting to relax more. At least he wasn't screaming. He didn't seem happy. But he did say that everything made sense. "I still think we're crazy," he said. "But it is a good plan."

Good that he was now a bit more positive. But at this point, I wasn't at all sure anymore. Now I was starting to feel a little panicked. Was thinking that this had to be the stupidest thing I'd ever thought of.

39

S o night fell, and Erika and I set off. We left at eight-thirty. The walk was only about fifteen minutes. But we wanted to make sure we weren't late.

It was kind of a strange walk, given the fact that we were about to meet a guy in league (in one way or another) with Belachek's murderer. Maybe more significant, I had kissed this woman last night.

I wanted to say something, since at this point in the day there had been no real acknowledgment of what had happened other than a brief smile in the morning. Frankly, other things had been on my mind. And Ruben had been with us. Kind of hard to juggle all these things. But now we had a little time, there were no prying ears, and I thought it might be good to get our mind off things. But what to say? That was the question. Finally, as we were crossing the river and after we had chatted a bit about Ruben's continual nervousness, I said, "You know, Erika, about last night." And then I paused, because I wasn't sure what to say next.

But Erika quickly jumped in. "Let's not talk about it," she said. "Not now. I can't think about it right now. Let's just get through all this. We'll talk when we get home."

"I wasn't really going to say anything," I continued. "I just wanted to say . . . ," and then I paused again because, in fact, I had no idea what I wanted to say.

Again, Erika turned to me and said, "Let's talk about this later, Evan. Now's not the right time."

And then I felt like crap because it hardly seemed like whatever she had to say could be good. The best it could be was neutral. That was the best. Very perplexing. And suddenly, as I considered all this, I became strangely and acutely aware of how I was about to meet my death at the Saint-Beauvais and all I could think about was a woman. A small version of my entire life, really. Pathetic.

Anyway, after idiotic and evasive small talk and a bit of wandering around in the neighborhood of the Saint-Beauvais, we arrived at the doorstep at exactly 9 p.m. The only good thing about this was that I quickly regained a better sense of how serious this all was and forgot about the previous night. And then, suddenly aware of just how crazy all this was, I said, "Just what the hell do we think we're doing?"

Erika looked at me and smiled. "This was your stupid idea," she said.

I paused for a second. But we were already at the entrance. Seemed too late to reconsider. I opened the door and stepped inside.

So things were a bit different at the Saint-Beauvais this time around. It's not like there were crowds of gangsters hunched over tables. Really wasn't at all like a secret hideout. And there wasn't anyone who looked like he was an international spy. I suppose one of the skinny Frenchmen sitting at the various tables could have been Lubchenko, but no one really struck me as an underworld type. The thing that was different was the way the owner acted. He smiled when he saw us and said, still in French, "It's very nice to see you both again." He had his clipboard in hand and again seemed to be adding up figures. But he put it aside and then said, "If you please, will you follow me?" And then he led us back through the kitchen.

Seems incredible to me now that we followed. But this guy was just so meek and kind. It just didn't seem possible that he'd be leading us to our deaths.

We walked past a fairly large butcher block counter and racks of iron pots and pans and then through another little hallway filled with shelves of dry food. Finally we arrived at a small door. The man knocked—three quick knocks—and then turned the door's handle and opened it. "He's just in there," he said to us. And then he looked at Erika and said, "I'm so sorry I was not frank with you the other day, mademoiselle."

Erika just smiled, too nervous to speak. Honestly, I was glad to see that she was a bit shaken, because I wanted company in what was now almost debilitating fear. I mean, who knew what was behind that door? Colburn with a big machine gun or a long, jagged knife? Could be. As we stepped forward past the owner, I just hoped Ruben executed the plan and called the cops if we didn't come back. Of course, if he was calling the cops, that meant we were in trouble, which was no good either. And for a brief second I thought about what being dead would be like.

And then I looked to my left and, for the first time, I saw Lubchenko.

40

The way Lubchenko looked was almost too perfect. He was something right out of a movie, which might be a boring way to describe someone, but it's a fact. He looked just exactly like you'd expect some sort of heroic and cinematic freedom fighter to look: well over six feet tall, enormous calloused hands, a huge handlebar mustache, a big chest with a large but manly stomach. His dark brown hair was combed back in a scattered but deliberate way, as though he had been up all night running his fingers through his hair as he looked over plans for a revolution. He also had scars on his face. Three. One that ran from the corner of his mouth to his chin. And two parallel scars just below his right eye. They were the kind of scars you'd be happy to have if you were staring down some other guy in a fight.

He was sitting at a table when we came in, but he quickly stood up when he saw us. "You must be Evan and Erika," he said. His English was excellent, but he spoke with what sounded like a Russian accent.

"Mr. Lubchenko," Erika said as she shook his hand.

"Yes," he replied. "But I should tell you that it's not my real name, so I don't care what you call me."

I wanted to say something at this point too. Needed to break the ice, so to speak. But I couldn't get anything out. Throat felt like it was filled with sand. I just shook Lubchenko's hand and nodded and looked around to see if there were any knives or guns lying about. Or even an angry Colburn hiding in the corner. All I saw was a desk, a laptop, a telephone, and stacks and stacks of papers. It looked more like an accountant's office than a hideout. I think that Lubchenko saw that I was casing the place, so he said, "You're safe. Colburn doesn't know that you're here. He doesn't even know that you're in Paris. Although he seems to think you might have a rather important laptop. It seems you have a criminal syndicate of your own, Mr. Macalister. This is what Colburn told me. But Colburn left for Seattle this afternoon. So you're safe for now." Lubchenko paused. Then he said, "Why don't we sit down?"

So we sat down, and a moment of silence passed. We all just kind of looked at each other for a few seconds while I thought about the implications of Colburn having found out about my theft from MRI. Very troubling, really. But I couldn't think about it for too long. In another second, Lubchenko began speaking again. "I would like to ask you to destroy that laptop when you get home, by the way. Erase the hard drive. I trust you know how to do that properly. I'll give you everything you need to replace it. In terms of evidence. To clear your father. But I'd like the laptop destroyed."

"Okay," I said, again as though sand were filling my throat.

"I assume that's why you came. To get what I promised Belachek?"

"Yes," Erika said. But she kind of had a slightly edgy tone. Then she said, "Why was Colburn here? Isn't he the one who killed Belachek? That's what your e-mail said."

Obviously Erika was a bit more articulate at this point, but I managed to speak up as well: "Our friend Ruben is waiting for us, and if you do anything to us, he'll know and go to the cops."

Pretty pathetic, really. But it's what came to mind.

Lubchenko didn't seem bothered. He just smiled. "Well, given the circumstances," he said, "you were smart to arrange that. But I assure you that I'm not going to hurt you. In fact, you're going to help me quite a bit. So I don't want you to get hurt.

"Colburn did kill Belachek," he continued. "Unfortunate. But a fact. And he was here because he thinks that I'm working with him. But I'm not. I'm working against him. I'm playing both sides, as it were. Which is why I'd very much like you to destroy the laptop when you return." Lubchenko smiled again and then said, "Although I can't say that I'm too worried about Colburn. Not personally, anyway. Ex-CIA operatives are a sharp, well-trained bunch. But you need to grow up under Soviet rule to be truly brutal. Like me." Lubchenko smiled broadly as he said this. "It's just that I'd like things to be as smooth as possible," he continued. "I always like for things to be smooth."

Pause. Then Erika said, "What exactly are we mixed up in? Why did Colburn kill Belachek?"

"Colburn killed Belachek for the same reason that he'll try to kill you if he ever finds out about this meeting. Or once he's sure that you have Belachek's laptop. He knew that Belachek was on to him. But he doesn't know that I set him up. He was here on other matters, although, again, he has no idea what's really going on." Lubchenko paused. "I'm sorry, but I actually don't have much time. I'll tell you what you need to know. But this will be brief.

"There's a small ring of people that Colburn is involved with that is selling live strains of the smallpox virus. That's at the heart of this. The FBI wasn't wrong about that. The only thing is that your father had nothing to do with it. He was, in fact, framed, as I'm sure you know. But things have spun out of control for Colburn, it seems. Too many people asking questions about smallpox. He's in a mess now. That's why he was here to see me."

Interesting, although I almost didn't want to hear any more.

"The people buying the smallpox strains," Lubchenko continued, "are people I'm involved with. Unfortunately. The organization started with good motives. I am, in fact, one of the people who started it. But now I'm trying to dismantle it. It's harder than you'd think, however. There's now lots of money involved. And when there's lots of money involved, things get fairly difficult."

"What's the organization?" Erika asked.

Again, I still wasn't really able to make any sort of sensible comment at this point.

"I come from a small nation in the Balkan region, which has basically been ruled over by outsiders for the past several hundred years," Lubchenko responded. "I think I'd prefer not to tell you its name. It's small, unimportant, and nobody really cares about it, except if you happen to be from there, in which case you probably care about it a great deal. At any rate, when we were still under Soviet control, and Bulgarian control, and Yugoslavian control, I started a small movement. The nation is in a remote part of the world. We were able to organize easily. And we were able to commit small disruptive acts that achieved little but made us feel good, I suppose. But when the Soviet Union fell, it really seemed like we might finally become a nation of our own. I guess it's what everyone in that part of the world wanted, or wants right now. The problem was we didn't get it. It's a small province, really. Not worth the time or energy of big nations. And we were no match for the kind of armies that surrounding nations were willing to throw against us.

"But we were well organized. This was a fact. And we had some money. And we were in close contact with other organizations in the region—people who wanted to establish homelands of *their* own. And before long, we were part of a coalition of what would now probably be called terrorists, although that word seems hardly to apply in any real sense.

"At any rate, I was for this coalition. I helped start it, in fact. Now I'm against it. That's all I can really say about that. The point with them now seems to be less the liberation of my nation and more the accumulation of wealth. People will pay money for all sorts of things these days. But a biological weapon, a weapon of mass destruction, is almost priceless. I don't know that the people from my organization would ever actually use such a weapon. I don't think so, at least. But they would be brokers. They would be willing to sell it—to raise money for the movement, they would say. Although at this point, that would be a lie. Their problem right now is not ideology or hostility. Their problem is greed.

"To make this simple, your father's company has live strains of smallpox, and my friends have connections with willing buyers. There's a lot of money to be made on this transaction. It's certainly why Colburn is involved. And it's why he took such extreme measures to silence Belachek and frame your father— he wanted Belachek dead without anyone suspecting that bigger things than blackmail were involved.

"My aim is simply to disrupt this transaction. And to do it as discreetly as possible, because I would prefer not to be discovered. Believe it or not, I still hold out hopes for my homeland. But get caught trafficking something like smallpox, and that hope is over. Countries like the United States, which has paid no attention to us at all, would certainly notice us then. And at that point, any hope of independence would be over for good."

Lubchenko paused as I tried to take all this in. Really heavy story. I was still speechless, although for different reasons now. I wasn't scared of Lubchenko so much as I was baffled by the depths of this whole situation. Just last night I had been totally distracted by trying to kiss one of my best friends. This was definitely a different kind of matter.

Lubchenko's pause stretched on, and when he opened his mouth to speak, he halted again. He looked pensive for another moment and then reached to his left and grabbed a box of latex gloves. "I believe I've told you what you need to know," he said. "Now put these gloves on. I want to give you something, but I don't think you should have your fingerprints on it."

He turned to a file cabinet to his left, opened it, and pulled out a large manila envelope.

"I think you'll find enough in here to free your father," he said. He opened the envelope and emptied its contents on a clean spot on his large wooden desk. He then went through the contents one by one.

It contained the following:

1. Several pictures of Colburn with what Lubchenko described as known terrorists. "The FBI will know these people immediately, so don't worry. But just in case, I've typed their names on the back of the photos." Lubchenko pointed to one of the photos containing badass-looking men. "These men," he said, "have just been arrested by the CIA with strains of smallpox virus that came from your father's company.

And I have something to go with this." (See number 2.)

2. Several records of account transfers from accounts belonging to each of these men into an account belonging to Colburn. The transactions were for eight million dollars. "There are more transactions," Lubchenko said. "More money. But these records will suffice."

3. A tape with what Lubchenko described as Colburn's lengthy description of how he killed Belachek and framed my father by planting phony e-mails and setting up the fake accounts. "This is the coup de grace," Lubchenko said. "Unassailable. Colburn, you must remember, has no idea that I was working with Belachek. I suggest you listen to this tape if you'd like to understand what kind of man you're dealing with. Colburn is normally fairly tight-lipped. But I needed him to assure me that he had taken care of everything properly. I am an important client of his."

4. Receipts of transfers from an account belonging to Colburn and the account in my father's name—the account that he apparently set up to prove that my father was embezzling money. There were no names on the receipts. Just numbers. But Lubchenko said that knowing the account numbers belonged to Colburn would allow the FBI to create a pretty solid paper trail.

"I think these items will clear things up for your father," Lubchenko said as he put the items back into the envelope.

"You'd better hope so, at least." He put the envelope into another envelope and said, "Again, I suggest you don't touch the inner envelope with your fingers."

Erika and I were speechless as we stared at Lubchenko and the envelope before us. What was there to say? Lubchenko smiled and said, "You know, to tell you the truth, I didn't quite know what I was going to do with all this. I was considering keeping it to myself after Belachek died. But our friend Mr. Colburn has been quite shrill lately, and I can't say I like it. I thought I might be able to manipulate him a little longer. He has contacts within my industry that even I don't have. But in my business, a shrill man is a dangerous man, and it made me somewhat nervous. I think at this point it's best to have him dealt with. That was the ultimate point, anyway. But I think it's better happening now rather than later."

Lubchenko paused for a second and then continued. "And to be honest," he said, "I didn't like the idea of your father being in jail unjustly. It wasn't going to change my decision. Injustice is a thing I see every day. You can't let it cloud your thinking. But I did feel sorry for him. I've been in jail before. Separated from my family. And I have a son, for that matter. I'm sure you've been a great comfort to your father. Obviously you're here for your own reasons. The laptop was quite a liability for you. But this took some bravery. And I'll tell you this: If you had turned over the laptop to the FBI, I would have disappeared immediately, as I now intend to do anyway. And without me, I guarantee that

Colburn would have gotten away with this. So, if you think about it, this little trip you've made is really the only way that your father would have gotten out of prison." I thought about this for a moment, and I have to say the idea kind of affected me.

Lubchenko paused again, and it seemed like he was getting ready to bring the meeting to an end, but I did have one final question.

"In your e-mail to Belachek," I said, "you mentioned that Mr. Richmond might be in on this, might have worked with Colburn. Is this true?"

Lubchenko hesitated for a moment. "That I still don't know," he finally said. "The only one who knows that is Colburn, and that is a secret he has kept very well. I'm sure if the FBI got hold of him, he'd talk. He's tough, but he's only interested in himself. I'm sure that if Richmond is in on it, he's probably pretty nervous that Colburn will get caught. Colburn has made a lot of enemies recently, and not many people think he's going to be above water for too much longer."

"Aren't *you* worried?" I asked.

"Well, Colburn has a problem. He doesn't really know who I am. Not really. Like I said, my name's not Lubchenko. It's just a name I borrowed from a very kind man who was the only one who could fix my old Mercedes, although the man is now dead and had nothing to do with any of this."

(That explained that.)

"As for my position here at Café Saint-Beauvais," Lubchenko

continued, "my assistant out there and I will be gone tonight. Anyway, Colburn has lost quite a bit of credibility with the people I'm involved with, and I don't think anyone will believe much of what he has to say. So, at this point, I'm more than happy to send Colburn away."

Lubchenko paused again and then stood up. "So, now," he said, "perhaps our business is done."

Erika and I stood up as well. Lubchenko stuck out his hand to Erika and shook it. And then he and I did the same. But as we began to shake, he held my hand tighter than I expected and pulled me closer to him. "My sense is that you will keep your mouth shut because you're in trouble yourself and wouldn't want anyone to know how you found out about me. That's one of the reasons I'm trusting you. I suggest you plant this evidence in Belachek's office. Make it look like it came from him, not from you. I'm sure you can handle that. My sense is that it's what you would have decided to do on your own. But just in case, I suggest again that you keep what was said here tonight a secret—no matter what kind of trouble you get in. I'm a resourceful man. Not the FBI, or the CIA, or anyone else would be able to protect you."

Again, the sand-in-the-throat thing. "I'll never say a word," I finally stammered. And I meant it.

41

As Erika and I left the Saint-Beauvais and headed back to the hotel, we were kind of giddy. We almost couldn't believe that we had survived or what we had just heard. It's really something to get that kind of a story from someone.

But as the walk progressed and Erika and I talked over what we had just heard, the giddiness and excitement began to give way. A couple of key facts kept glaring out at us. (1) We were carrying information that could send a very dangerous man to jail, and (2) this man was already on to us—he already suspected that we might have a laptop that could lead us to Lubchenko. It seemed like we were going to pull this off. It seemed like we could get Lubchenko's envelope back to Seattle and bust Colburn. But there was a lot at stake. And there was a lot that could go wrong.

We got back to the Crillon at ten-ten, well within the allotted time. Ruben was relieved to see us, although he looked like he had really sweated the last hour.

"It looks like Colburn went back to Seattle today," I said. "So I think we can relax a bit. But only a bit. He might have changed his mind."

"Great," Ruben said, clearly nervous. "So it's only slightly possible that we may die tonight. But what happened with Lubchenko?"

"It's actually a pretty incredible story," I said, and then we all sat down on the couches in front of the fire and Erika and I told him what we'd heard.

It was about eleven when we came to the end of the story (Ruben, needless to say, was blown away), and now we were all left wondering what was next.

We decided that we shouldn't take any chances. We wanted to go out since it was our last night in Paris. But since we hadn't actually seen Colburn get on the plane, we decided it was best to lie low.

The one small business matter we had to take care of was what to do with the evidence once we got it back to Seattle. There were a few options, including just mailing it. I had the card of that FBI agent at home—Agent Diaz—and I could just send it to him anonymously.

"The problem is how long it might take," I said.

"Yeah, we need Colburn taken care of right away," Ruben said. "Hate the idea of relying on the mail. And then who knows how long it will sit unopened on someone's desk."

Anyway, we decided that the evidence would be promptly attended to (and most convincing) if it looked like it came right from Belachek's office—like Lubchenko had suggested. So the plan was for me to go into MRI the next day, go to Belachek's office, move around a few cabinets and files, and then walk out, saying I'd found the envelope behind a bookcase. Yes, it would look a bit fishy. Very fishy, maybe. But if they asked me what I had been doing in there, I'd just claim to be a desperate son grasping at straws, trying to help his father. It was true that the cops had turned the office inside out. They'd definitely wonder how they missed it and how I found it. Would be almost unbelievable. I was sure they wouldn't believe it at first. But the evidence seemed so solid that I figured they'd forget about me soon enough—once they validated its authenticity. Remember, I was the dopey son who couldn't even pass algebra. It was quite a cover. They might think it was suspicious, but what would be the alternative theories—that I had flown to Paris and met with the leader of a revolutionary group who gave me the envelope?

"Anyway," Ruben added as we finally agreed on this plan, "the FBI won't be into making a big deal about how they missed evidence. They'll probably try to keep it quiet. I can't imagine them wanting to highlight something they might have overlooked."

The plan wasn't ideal, but it was the best we could come up with.

The one other thing we decided was that we'd all spend the night at my house when we got back to Seattle. We were safer together than apart. We'd get to Seattle, Erika and Ruben would go home to check in with their free-thinking parents, and then they'd come over. I have to say that made me feel good. I really didn't like being alone in the same city as Colburn. He really was the main danger at the moment. Kind of frightening.

Anyway, like I said, we were tired. So once we had solidified the plan, we went to sleep.

S o, we were still a long way from done. In
fact, we were probably never more threat-
ened as we were on the day we headed back to
Seattle. There was a killer on the loose, and he
was starting to catch on to what we were doing.

But there was an end in sight, and the route was
at least plain to us now, even if it would be hard to
follow. Strangely, though, for that whole day—checking out of
the hotel, wandering around Charles de Gaulle Airport, getting
on the plane, getting off the plane—I felt very, very disoriented.
And by the time we were walking through the Seattle airport,
my vague kind of confusion had only increased. It was hard to
put my finger on it. But by eight that night, as we were riding in
a cab back to my neighborhood in Seattle, I started feeling very
lonely and very sad about going back to an empty house.

I missed my mother. Something that happens very intensely
from time to time. And I was suddenly thinking very hard about
my father. I kind of hated him—that was true. But for some reason I also had a pretty big urge to visit him in jail the next
morning and tell him everything that had happened—that I had
been to Paris, tracked down Lubchenko, and gotten the evidence that was going to set him free. I guess it wasn't over yet.

But I had done pretty well, despite the various hang-ups. I don't know. Most of my life my father treated me like I was a total fool and a total idiot. I think I just wanted to tell him what I'd done in order to prove him wrong, to make him feel like he had misjudged me. I wanted to impress him. But I also think, maybe, that I wanted to show him that he could count on me. I kept thinking about what Lubchenko said—how he would have disappeared if I had turned over the laptop and my father would never have gotten out of prison. Lubchenko had been right that I had my own reasons to keep the laptop to myself— that I wanted to keep my theft racket a secret. But I couldn't help but also feel like I had done something to help my father. Even if it wasn't entirely for the right reasons. When my father treated me like I was an idiot, I have to say that lots of times it seemed like he was right. As must be obvious, I can be pretty stupid. And maybe the trip to Paris was its own kind of stupidity. But I had done something. I had achieved something. And I kind of wanted my father to know. Whatever. All sentimental crap that I normally don't indulge in. But this was what was on my mind, I guess.

But most on my mind, for some reason, was what my father and I went through when my mother died. I thought about my father sitting in the federal building in downtown Seattle, and how alone he was, and then how alone he was when my mother died, and how her death pretty much wrecked our own already-troubled relationship. Lubchenko said that he was sure

I was a source of great comfort to my father. But as the cab wound its way through Seattle, it occurred to me that I had never really been a source of comfort to anyone. Certainly not my father, and certainly not when he needed me the most—in jail, and after my mother passed away.

One of the tougher things about my mother's death, I think, was that she died of cancer—of the liver—the thing that my father's company made millions of dollars curing. I'd say it's ironic, but it's hard to perceive irony when it's you that a thing has happened to. It's just very tragic and very hard to think about. I know it's kept my dad up at nights. It kept him up when my mother first got sick. It kept him up when she first went to the hospital. And it kept him up when we finally under-stood that she was never coming home. My dad knows every-one in the medical industry—famous doctors, genius scientists, hospital presidents. He's friends with or has met almost all of them. And when my mom got sick, he called everybody there was. And he got a lot of help—lots of people pitched in and tried to help my mother. But in the end, none of it did any good. Cancer is a very democratic disease. And being rich and connected—even being a cancer doctor—doesn't help. And after it's over, none of the things that you have provide any comfort at all. The fact is that it's a thing that you never get over. You really don't. Whatever. I think my dad was a lonely man, and going back to the empty house, I felt lonely too, and maybe what I was thinking most was that it really sucked that my father and I were never able to turn to each other to deal with this loneliness.

I thought about these things quite a bit as the cab got closer to my house. And as we pulled onto my street, I really thought I ought to make more of an effort after all this, that I needed to be a better son. My dad would be home from prison soon enough. I'd make sure of that. And then maybe things might be different. Maybe he'd be more relaxed with me. Maybe I wouldn't be such a cutup.

And then I thought about all the times I had had these thoughts and how they never came true. And again, I wished I wasn't headed home to an empty house.

43

As the cab pulled in front of my house, I began to regain a sense of what was immediately at stake. Felt like I was waking up from something. Erika and Ruben had been silent this whole time as well. We were all just tired, I think. Still, things had to get kicked up a notch now that we were back. We were still in danger.

I fumbled for the door handle and then opened the taxi door. Ruben and Erika followed me out. We paid the driver and then walked to Erika's car, which was still parked outside my house.

We stood silently for a moment, then I forced a smile and said, "You guys know the plan?"

"I'll be over in half an hour," Ruben said.

"I'll be a bit longer," Erika said. "About an hour. But I'll be there soon."

"Just let's all be careful," I replied. They both nodded and climbed in the car. I turned and headed up the path toward my house.

I was still thinking about my father and my mother, but as I typed in the security code on our alarm system and entered my house, I have to say that my dominant feeling definitely changed to fear. Who knew what Colburn would be up to now? And if he had figured out my little theft ring, I wouldn't be too surprised if he was on his way to figuring out the Paris trip. Still, I hoped I had some time. Even the most connected criminals can't work that fast.

When I got inside, I flipped on as many lights as possible and turned on a basketball game in the TV room for a little background noise. As part of my initial lie, I had told Mrs. Andropolis that we were driving down from the cabin the next day, so I didn't really expect her. Just as well, as far as I was concerned. Still, again, I was feeling lonely and fairly creeped out.

I decided that I'd make the best of things, though. Ruben and Erika would come over. The alarm system would be on. We'd load up some of my dad's guns. And then we'd sleep in my dad's study till the morning, when I could bring the goods on Colburn to Belachek's office and pretend to find them.

All very simple.

Really. Very simple.

An ironclad plan.

And then Ruben called.

When I heard his voice, I felt kind of sick. It was that initial high pitch. Made me think he wasn't coming over—that he'd feel safer at home, that he didn't want to get into any more trouble.

Exhausting.

But what he said made me realize that things were much, much more serious. Much, much worse.

"The laptop is gone," he said.

"What?" I replied.

"Belachek's laptop is gone. Someone busted into the garage. They took the laptop."

"Was it your parents?"

"The lock and door handle are broken, Evan."

"Have your parents seen it?"

"I don't think so. They haven't said anything. It must have happened in the past day. My parents would have noticed by now otherwise."

"Was anything else taken?"

"Nothing."

"Look, come over. We'll decide what to do from here."

"This is a major problem, Evan. It's Colburn. It couldn't be anyone else."

"I know. I know. Just come over."

"He'll know what we know as soon as he turns the computer on. Everything's been cracked into. And I'm sure he's the one that planted the stroke recorder. It will take him a half hour to know what we've been doing. He'll go online and find our flight records. He'll find our hotel records. He'll know when we got home tonight."

"Ruben, I understand. Just come over. We're safer here. We'll deal with it from here."

"We've got to go to the police, Evan."

"Okay. Ruben. Okay. I'm not saying no. But let's talk. I've

got the alarm on. We're totally safe. You know the code. Just come in. I'll be in my dad's study with the guns. We can call the police from here if we decide to. I'm not saying no to that. But let's not do anything until we talk."

There was a pause. Ruben was hesitating.

"We need to talk," I said. "Come over. We're safest here."

Again, there was a pause. Then, "I'll be over in five minutes."

"Be careful," I said. And then we hung up.

44

I immediately went to check the alarm again and then headed to my dad's study. Let me say that I know nothing about guns, and my dad sure as hell didn't teach me anything. "You're never putting your mitts on these, boy," he often said. "At least not till I'm dead." Funny guy. Why did I feel sad about us not getting along better?

Anyway, like I've already said, my dad kept the guns locked up. In a huge gun safe. Very responsible. Fortunately, I knew where all my dad's keys were hidden. A teenager can always outsmart an elderly father. He actually had a whole ring of keys that he kept in an old leather-covered box in the study closet. I went to the study, opened the closet, grabbed the keys, and in another minute I was looking at about twenty guns—all of various sizes and shapes, meticulously lined up in the safe.

The thing is that I really had no idea how to use one. Sure, simple enough: aim and pull the trigger. But first you had to load them. And there were boxes and boxes of bullets of all different sizes. Also, some of the guns only carried one or two bullets. If I was going to be in a gunfight, I wanted something with lots of bullets. I've seen too many movies where the good guy's gun empties before the bad guy gets whacked. And some of the guns were antiques. Didn't know if I should use those. Didn't know if they'd work right.

Of course, the plan was for none of this stuff to be necessary. But Colburn now had the laptop. He might not understand everything at first. But he was a smart guy. And we couldn't take any chances. Ruben and I were going to load a bunch of guns and sit up all night or until we could figure out what to do. I have to admit that even I was now thinking about calling the FBI. I mean, I've done a lot of stupid things in my life. But hiding out in my dad's study with a bunch of guns really takes the cake. It would be my all-time-stupidest stunt.

Still, knowing full well that something is stupid has never stopped me before.

Suddenly I heard a noise at the front entryway. It was faint, but I thought it was the front door. Must be Ruben. Five minutes had passed since he called. Had to be him. Still, I was kind of freaked out.

"Ruben?" I yelled.

A second passed.

"Ruben," I said again. Again, we had a big house, and it's kind of a walk from the front door to the study.

Then, in another second, in Ruben's typical scratchy, nervous voice, I heard, "It's me, Evan."

"I'm in the study," I replied.

"Everything is A-OK," he yelled.

"Okay," I said, kind of distracted by the guns again. And

then a kind of chill hit me, although I wasn't sure why. I stepped back from the gun case and looked at the door. I wanted Ruben to get there. We'd lock up. We'd load the guns. And then we'd be safe. We'd stay up all night. We'd talk things over. And in the morning, we'd get the evidence to the FBI and bust Colburn.

Still, I was suddenly very nervous.

I just wanted to see Ruben.

And then there he was. At the door.

There was a sudden rush of relief. Was almost funny, really. I thought about it for a brief instant. This scrawny kid would never save me from anything. But I was so glad to see him. And then he looked at me funny. He always looked scared out of his wits. But now he really looked scared. White as a sheet. Looked like he was going to vomit.

"We'll be all right, Ruben," I said. "We'll be all right."

Ruben just looked at me with these sad, worried eyes. He looked at me. Then he stepped forward. And then from the side, behind the doorway, his gun raised to Ruben's head, stepped Colburn.

Suddenly I remembered the A-OK signal from Paris. But it was too late.

C olburn had a kind of inhuman look to him.  **45**
Like he couldn't be reasoned with. He was
like a shark or an alligator—no mind, no emo-
tion, just a sort of killing machine. This wasn't a
guy who was going to spare our lives because we
were kids. This was pretty much it.

"Hello, Evan," Colburn said, almost casually. "It's
time to put an end to all this, I think."

I stepped back. There had to be some way out. And then, at
that moment, I saw something else that made my blood run
even colder. I had stepped back to the other side of the room. I
was at the window and I could see the front of the house—the
study kind of bent off to the side. And there, just arriving at the
front door, was Mr. Richmond. The door had been left slightly
ajar. In the next instant, Richmond disappeared inside.

I had to think quick. "If you kill us, you're screwed," I blurted
out. "People will figure out what happened." I might not get
sympathy from Colburn, but there was always self-interest.

But Colburn quickly corrected me. "Wrong, kiddo," he said.
"Killing you is the best thing I can do at this point. But I'll make
it painless, so there's nothing to worry about."

"Two dead sixteen-year-old kids and the whole game

changes," I said. "You'll get caught for this. The cops will figure it out."

"I'll have to take my chances."

"We won't say anything."

Colburn laughed at this. "You're going to let your dad rot in jail? I don't think so."

I tried to think of something else to say, but I was running out of arguments. I really wished that I had loaded a gun at that point. Ruben was close to the safe. But his head was also inches away from the barrel of Colburn's pistol. He'd have to be Batman to get a gun, load it, and get off a shot. Not possible. And not possible for me. And then there was Mr. Richmond. My mind raced with the implications of him being here. Almost too much to bear. I was about to die and was still trying to figure everything out. And there was poor Ruben, gun to his head, looking at me with the saddest, most frightened eyes I had ever seen.

Suddenly there was a shot. Then another. I ducked. Fell to the floor. But I kept my eyes open. I watched. I watched as Ruben fell to the floor. Fell at the same time I did.

But so did Colburn. It was a confusing scene. A spray of blood covered the white couch against the wall. We were all on the ground. And standing behind us, with his stupid-ass silvery gun in his hand, was Mr. Richmond. He was just standing there, shaking.

"Ruben!" I screamed out, suddenly coming to my senses.

He lay still, in front of me, but then looked up. His eyes were glassy—totally terrified. He had blood on his face and neck. But he was moving. Then he said, "I think I'm okay. I don't think I was hit."

And then I looked past him and saw Colburn lying on the ground. His body was twitching—twitching in the most horrible way. His head was half crushed. An eye, and a cheek, and part of his forehead were missing. Blood flowed from the wound. The glistening gray of his brain throbbed. It was Colburn that had been shot.

I looked up at Richmond, who had now lowered his gun and was just staring at the scene before him. He looked terrified himself. The hand that held his gun was shaking. The muscles in his face were recoiled, frozen in terror.

Richmond had saved us.

So he wasn't in on it, I thought. And then something else occurred to me as I lay on the floor—something Lubchenko said: if Richmond *had* been involved in all this, he must have been nervous about Colburn getting caught and fingering him. And, conveniently, he had just killed Colburn.

I stared at Richmond for a moment. Richmond just kept looking at Colburn. And then, he turned his head and looked at me. We just stared at each other for a moment. Eye to eye.

Richmond didn't look like Colburn had. There wasn't that inhuman stare. There wasn't that cold look of a man who could kill without pity. Still, what did that mean? Can you really tell what someone is like just by staring into his eyes? And then, finally, after another instant, Richmond turned away.

In a shaking voice he said, "I just came by to check on you. He had a gun. I thought he was going to kill you. I don't understand what's going on. What was he doing?" Richmond put the gun in his arm holster and ran his fingers through his hair. He was really shaken—that was no act. But that didn't make his explanation any more true. And then he said, "I should call the police." He pulled out his cell phone and moved into the hallway.

Ruben slowly moved forward and curled into a crouched position. He didn't want to turn around to see the body. But he was covered with blood. He kind of moved forward now, toward me. I thought he might start to cry. But he held it together. "What now?" he finally whispered.

It was a puzzle. But it's surprising how alert your mind is in these situations. My brain raced through the possibilities. Finally I said, "If we come clean now, we'll be finished. We're in too deep. We need to just shut up for right now. Don't say anything. No matter what anybody asks. We don't know why he was here. The cops won't understand. But I can't plant the envelope in Belachek's office now. I'll just put it in the mail tomorrow. The FBI will have it in two days. They'll put it together. Then they'll think that Colburn was here to do more damage to my father and that we surprised him. That's what they'll think. It will confuse them at first. But when they get the envelope, they'll put it together. So for now, say nothing. We know nothing, Ruben. Nothing."

46

The rest of that night is still kind of a blur. Everything happened so fast. But the adrenaline that shoots through you at such a moment is incredible. And Ruben and I managed to keep our game faces on.

Erika arrived to a gruesome scene. She had thought we were going to stay up that night. Play cards. Load guns. Keep an eye out for bad guys. She didn't expect to find Colburn shot in the head.

I managed to intercept her before she saw too much. Cops were now combing the place, trying to figure out what had happened. When I saw her, I quickly pulled her aside and gave her the instructions I gave Ruben. "Just keep quiet. Say nothing. Let the evidence we have do the talking. I'll get it to the FBI anonymously. In a few days, they'll draw their own conclusions. Then we'll be out of this mess. But for now, say absolutely nothing."

Fortunately, the cops didn't question Erika. Why would they? She hadn't been there. Unfortunately, they gave Ruben and me the third degree. Both at the house and then down at the police station. But they questioned us together. That was good. We stuck together and stayed strong. And we really didn't have too much to hide. We didn't do any shooting. We weren't threatening anyone. We didn't sneak into somebody else's house. And the cops didn't really ask the right questions. They wanted to know why we thought Coburn was there. But when we said we had no idea, they kind of bought it. I mean, what possible reason could there be? That we had unmasked him as an international terrorist trafficking weapons of mass destruction? We were two scrawny kids, scared out of our minds and clearly too stupid to know anything at all.

Still, it was hard. It was hard sitting there talking to the cops, saying over and over that we didn't know anything. It felt like our lies were just getting deeper and deeper. And the deeper they got, the more we had to find a way out. If our cover was blown now, we really would be dead. There's only so much you can lie and steal and cheat before they really send you up for a long time.

But the questioning ended. For that night, at least. Or morning. It was 2 a.m. when things broke up. And since Ruben and I weren't actually accused of doing anything wrong—no one even suspected such a thing, as far as I can tell—we were simply turned loose. Needless to say, Ruben's parents were at the police station waiting for him. They might be liberal, easygoing parents, but when you find out that your son has witnessed a murder, you worry. Even my dad worried. I got word of that from one of the cops. "We told your old man you were in some trouble," he said.

"How did he take it?" I asked.

"Well, he was concerned. But then he said it figured. Guy's kind of a grouch, huh?" The cop smiled. Again, have a dad like mine, and people feel sorry for you. And to be honest, the cops just felt sorry for us generally. We had witnessed something pretty terrible.

Anyway, I left Ruben and I left the police station having been absolutely no help to anyone. Everyone was stumped. What was Colburn doing at my house? Nobody knew. It must have crossed somebody's mind that this might have something to do with my dad's case. But there was just so little to go on that I think they really didn't know what to make of it. Then again, they weren't going to tell me anything. I was just some dopey kid who had nothing to do with anything.

Ruben's parents gave me a ride home, and when we arrived at my house, Mrs. Andropolis was there, along with a bunch of cops again. I was actually happy to see her and gave her a huge hug. But then I suddenly became panicked that one of these nosy cops was going to find the Colburn envelope, and before talking too much, I ran to my room to make sure it was still safe. And there it was, in my beat-up backpack, in the corner of the room, lying on top of a pile of dirty clothes. The perfect hiding place. What cop would think to look there for anything important? After that, I went back down to see Mrs. Andropolis. I needed serious sympathy. It had been a hard week. And I still wasn't out of the woods yet.

"You poor, poor boy," she said when she saw me. "This is a

madhouse. It's just so upsetting. You shouldn't have seen any of these things." Then she asked me if I was hungry. It was now two-thirty in the morning. But I didn't quite feel like going to bed at that moment.

"Maybe I'll just have a bowl of ice cream," I said.

"Yes," she said. "Have some ice cream."

A few cops were still hanging around. But most were on their way out. Everything in the study had been taped off. And by the time I had a bowl of ice cream in front of me, I was alone in the kitchen with Mrs. Andropolis. Good thing. Like I said, I needed attention. And again, I still wasn't out of trouble yet.

47

S o, I had one task the next morning. Mail the Colburn evidence to Agent Diaz at the FBI. And then pray. I had to do a lot of praying. And pleading. And selling my soul. The evidence had to register with them. If it didn't, I was going to have to come forward.

I put on gloves to conceal my fingerprints and wrote Diaz's address on the front of the envelope. I disguised my handwriting as much as possible, although I didn't imagine anyone would suspect that it had come from me. I also included a short note. It said, *I think that this will change your mind about the Macalister case.* I signed it, *A friend.* After that, I walked it down to the main post office and dropped it in the mail. Between what was going on with my father, the fact that Colburn had been killed, and the evidence that Diaz would now have, I figured it was going to get sorted out. If it wasn't, I'd just bite the bullet and go forward with the story of what I had been through. But first I was going to wait. Had to give it some time.

In the next week, Ruben and I were questioned three more times. They were intense questionings—with both of us in the room and then separately. I managed to keep my mouth shut.

And so did Ruben. Good news. I know they were questioning Mr. Richmond too. I saw him at the police station more than once. Every time he just smiled and said, "Don't worry, big guy, we just have to let the cops do their jobs." But they let him go, just like us—and he had actually killed a man.

Mr. Richmond had three lawyers in tow. And his explanation was convincing. He had stopped by to check on me and found a crazed man about to shoot a sixteen-year-old kid in the head. What was he supposed to do? And he had a license to carry the weapon. And lots of training. What was the gun for if not to take out a deranged lunatic? It was a solid story.

Anyway, the questioning all progressed smoothly. Colburn was the only bad guy in their eyes (although they had no idea what he was up to), and none of the questions got at all aggressive with Ruben and me. And we really managed to shut up. We didn't say a thing. Nobody was doubting our innocent confusion. Still, as the days passed, I started sweating the situation more and more, mostly because nothing changed with my dad's case. I think I had half expected the mayor of Seattle to go on national TV one day to announce that they had made a terrible mistake and that they were going to have a big parade in my dad's honor. But several days passed, and nothing happened. And I kind of started freaking out again. Would I still have to come forward to confess everything—even after all that had happened? How much longer was this going to go on?

But then, finally, after what felt like way, way too long, I got good news. And it actually did come over the TV. It wasn't the mayor. But it was a spokesman from the FBI. He was giving a news conference when I flipped on the television. Apparently, there had been a breakthrough with the Macalister case. New evidence had been uncovered. The murder of Belachek had not been committed by Macalister. It had been committed by another man—a man whose name was being withheld because of security concerns. And that evening, before Mrs. Andropolis had finished cooking dinner, my father walked through the door.

Y ou might imagine that a homecoming of this sort would warrant all sorts of wild celebration, cheers, hugging, etc., etc. It would in most families. It seemed like forever since my dad was first carted off, and I'm pretty sure it felt the same for my dad as well. The truth is that we almost didn't survive it. We very nearly lost everything.

All the same, as might be expected, my dad handled his return like a tough guy. He came through the door—now in a blue suit rather than the orange prison uniform—and just kind of nodded very matter-of-factly to me and Mrs. Andropolis. "Evan. Mrs. Andropolis," he said. "I assume you've heard the news. If not, as you can now see, I'm free and I've returned home."

I stood up as he stepped into the middle of the kitchen, and I think I still half expected some kind of burst of emotion, some kind of joyful hug. But he was still several feet away from me, and he merely turned to Mrs. Andropolis to ask her when dinner would be ready. After she told him that it would be ready in about ten minutes, he said, "Well, then, I think I'd like to take a quick shower," and then he headed up the stairs.

Mrs. Andropolis looked at me out of the corner of her eye. It was a look that I knew well. The truth is that despite her bossy behavior, she was actually very fond of my father. She had real affection for the guy, as much as she tried to hide it. But I don't think she liked his brusque attitude with me. I think she thought there ought to be something more than a nod between the two of us. Still, she was also pretty smart. She just looked at me and said, kind of quietly, "Oh, yeah, sure, big man not happy to be home. I'll bet. You just remember, Evan, that his acts don't mean anything. He's happy. You trust me. He's happy. Very happy." And then she smiled at me.

I wasn't so sure. My dad's a tough guy, and just because almost every other person on the planet would be overjoyed on such an occasion didn't mean that he would be.

Still, it's a fact that I also wasn't racing to him with open arms. I didn't make a move to give him a big hug any more than he did, and as he came back downstairs and sat down at the large granite table in our kitchen, I began to feel a bit guilty. I just didn't understand why it was all so hard—especially now. But it was.

Mrs. Andropolis put a big bowl of beef and vegetables on the table and then a big plate of Greek flat bread, and then she said she had some chores in the basement. She was being much quieter than usual, and I think she wanted to give us some time alone. It made sense, but as we both began putting food onto our plates, I kind of started dreading sitting there and making small talk, pretending that my father hadn't just been sent to prison and that I hadn't just seen a man shot in the head.

But it didn't take more than a bite before my dad broke the awkwardness. He did it in a direct, no-nonsense, Lutheran, northern Minnesotan way. He ripped a piece of bread in half, dipped it into the sauce from the beef, and said that he was, in fact, sorry for what I had gone through. He kind of paused at that point, and I half expected some kind of abstract tale from his youth that might illustrate the importance of honesty and hard work. But then his eyes kind of moistened, and he kind of smiled, and he turned his head to me and said, "It's kind of a commonplace thing to say, but it's also true, so I'll say it: life can get pretty hard, Evan. It can get pretty hard. We just have to remember to stick together. We have to remember that you and I have to stick together. No matter what. And there's nothing as important as that. Not MRI, not this house, nothing. We've always got to stick together."

I didn't know what to say. I didn't have much experience with this kind of talk. "Okay, Dad," I said.

"You'll remember that?" he said.

"I'll remember that," I said, and for a second the whole trip to Paris kind of flashed before my eyes, and I suddenly wanted to tell him everything. It seemed like I could, like I could tell him the whole story and that he'd be amazed that I was still alive, and that I had seen so many things, and that I had been able to cover so much ground so quickly, and that I was the one that got him out of prison. But this was just an idea, just a momentary notion, and in the next second I decided that it was still a story that was best kept to myself. It occurred to me that I'd probably never have the kind of open relationship that some kids have with their parents. But that had more to do with my dad's character than with his feelings. I think the best you can hope for with my dad is a few moments of connection. My dad had limitations—he had a limited way of dealing with the world and with me. But in some ways, despite the obvious restraint, those few moments of connection suddenly seemed like a lot to me. They seemed like a lot. And what my father had just said to me seemed like a lot as well. I just hoped that I could keep up my end—that I wouldn't let him down so much.

My father looked at me for another moment, smiled, and then began scooping a big piece of meat onto his bread. His eyes were still kind of teary. But he held it together. He lifted the bread to his mouth, began chewing, and then said that the food at the jail had been absolutely miserable and that he was most happy to be back because of "Mrs. Andropolis's magnificent cooking." And then he smiled again, and I realized (perhaps with some relief) that the emotional odyssey of the last minute and a half was now at an end.

S o, in the spirit of my father—and to prove that I am, in fact, my father's son—I just need to resolve my story a bit further and take you away from the wild emotional excesses of our first meal back together.

A crisis puts lots of things in perspective. But it's funny how in the midst of life-and-death situations, the mind can still return to mundane matters. And I have to say that with the exception of the moment I was lying next to Colburn's dead body, the matter of Erika and me never really disappeared completely from my consciousness. And the day after my father came home, as I walked Erika home from Ruben's house and we talked about all that had happened, that strange kiss in the hall of the Ritz was still on my mind. I wanted to bring up the matter but was afraid to, for all the reasons I'm always afraid to talk about such things. Rejection, humiliation, ridicule, etc., etc. I had to get home that night anyway. Mrs. Andropolis was making a sort of Greek suckling pig for my father and me, and I promised I wouldn't be late. *Later,* I told myself. *I'll deal with the Erika thing later.* And in that way, I really felt like things were getting back to normal.

As we got close to Erika's house, though, she kind of

stopped talking and started looking a little nervous. And then, just as we got to the edge of her driveway, she stopped, looked at me for a moment, and then asked me what I thought about us kissing in Paris. "I mean, what happened there?" she said.

Quickly, I offered a thoughtful account of my actions. "It was a mistake," I said. "Just a drunken mistake. I don't know why it happened. But I'm really sorry."

She just looked at me and smiled. "Evan, you're an idiot," she said.

"A total idiot," I agreed. "A complete idiot."

"Look," she continued. "To be honest . . . I think I liked it. I liked the kiss. And I think . . . I think I want to kiss you again."

Pause. I didn't know what to say to this. Never heard anything like this before.

Then she stepped forward, put her hand on my face, and kissed me again. Lasted a few seconds. Maybe more. Maybe twenty seconds. I don't know. Then she pulled away, smiled, and said, "Okay. Get home to dinner. But call me afterward? Maybe you can come over and we can study together tonight." She looked at me for another second, then turned and headed up to her house.

"Okay," I eventually said, trying to regain my composure. "I'll come over tonight to study." She turned again, smiled at me again, and then went into her house.

Shocking. All very shocking. I don't even know what else to say about that. And what happened that evening is nobody's business. But it was a beginning of something. Something. I will say that.

And now, one final thing about my father.

About a week after my dad got home, a very damaging piece of mail arrived at our house. My dad said nothing about it at first, but after doing a little investigating on his own, he called me into his study—the one with the guns—and had me sit down in front of him at his desk. He then smiled and placed before me his credit card bill.

"I want you to tell me about this," he said, his voice now barely restraining his anger. "And I want you to tell me everything. I want to know why you went to Paris, why you stayed at the Ritz, why you ate a hundred and fifty dollars' worth of Chinese food, and"—here my dad began to stutter, and when he got through the stutter, he began to scream—"and why in God's name you booked four separate rooms in one night including a suite at the Crillon for four thousand dollars." As he said "four thousand dollars," he began banging his fist on the desk, and grimacing, and kicking the floor. "Why, why, why, why, why?"

I was kind of speechless. Very hard to answer someone when they're speaking to you that way. But he decided to answer his own question. "Old man is in jail, so time to do a little celebrating? Time to have a little fun? Have a little holiday? Take his credit card and have a little party in Europe? Take your idiot friends on a little vacation? Don't deny it, Evan. I know you did it. Do not sit here and try to deny this."

Now, let me just say that in this particular kind of situation, I've found, over the years, that it's always, always best to lie. It's sometimes tempting to tell the truth. You think that maybe this time it's best to just come clean and make up. But this is never, ever true. You should never, ever do this, even if you've just had a discussion with the person about how from here on out you're going to "stick together." I simply furrowed my brow, turned the bill around to face me, looked at the various entries for a moment, and said, "Dad, I have no idea who did this. It must have been Colburn when he was setting you up."

When I said this, my dad's fist came down on his desk faster and harder than even I thought it could. "I know you did it. Don't tell me that. I have proof. I have proof you did it."

This, of course, was impossible. I had thought of the angles and was quite sure that he had nothing close to proof. This conclusion, however, was false. It's amazing how much you can forget when someone's trying to kill you. I just had not been at the top of my game. Hadn't, in fact, covered all the bases, as they say. My dad looked at me for a moment, smiled maliciously, then reached below his desk and picked up a large but previously hidden leather elephant-shaped footstool. The one the luggage store didn't have in stock—the one I had to get delivered.

"I assume you recognize this, Evan," he said. "It came yesterday. And I've got the receipt—the same receipt that has the seven-hundred-and-fifty-dollar suitcase on it. And you may have forged my signature. But they kept the delivery form you filled

out, and that address is definitely written in your handwriting."
My dad was now waving around the delivery form, and, I will
add, smiling like a kid on his birthday. Really. I don't think I've
ever seen him this happy. I mean, he loved this. He loved bust-
ing me. Nothing in the world made him as happy. It seemed to
prove all his worst suspicions of me and that he was somehow a
cunning, genius father. Really. I thought he was going to start
leaping up and down at this point, he was so happy.

"And now, my boy, what I'd like to see is this seven-
hundred-and-fifty-dollar suitcase you bought. It must be a real
beauty. I can't wait to lay my eyes on that one."

At this point, decision making was a bit tougher. It seemed
to me that I had been caught, although this certainly didn't pre-
clude continuing to deny everything. I've denied worse. I've
denied plenty of things I've been caught doing red-handed. It's
part of my lifestyle.

Still, since I was busted one way or another, and it didn't
seem like there was any way out, and because I suddenly
started feeling pissed off with my father (because why the hell
did he always have to yell at me like this?), I also thought that
there was the obnoxious-answer option. I mean, I didn't even
have the suitcase anymore. I left it behind at the Ritz when
Colburn was thinking about putting a bullet between my eyes
as I was trying to save my father's ass. But my dad was pretty
adamant. He wanted to see that suitcase. Kept screaming that
he wanted to see that "seven-hundred-and-fifty-dollar suitcase

that my darling son has seen fit to buy himself." And it was just all so boring and obnoxious for me to listen to that I finally just said, "I'm sorry, Dad, but I can't show it to you. I accidentally left it at the Ritz."

And then the fist came down again on the desk and he just started screaming again. "You're grounded," he said. "Grounded. You're never allowed out again. And you're going to pay me back every single penny of this. Do you hear me, boy?"

Anyway, it went on for some time like this, and I just sat there politely, listening to all the things that were going to happen to me. What else was I going to do?

I did wonder again, though, what it would be like to tell my dad what had happened. How he might react if I explained how I stole office equipment from MRI, how I had withheld key evidence in his case, how I went to Paris to get the goods on Colburn, how I did a million other things that he'd never believe in a million years. Maybe he'd get more furious. Probably. But maybe he might develop some kind of new respect for me. Puzzling.

But again, in these situations, it's always best to keep your mouth shut, no matter how close a guy tells you he wants to be with you. My dad meant it when he said we had to stick together. I'm sure it was honest, and true, and that he meant it. I know it. But if I told him the real story of all that had happened, he'd still have my head. Seemed best to let him think that I was the delinquent kid who ran off to Paris for a vacation.

Not that far from the truth. I was a delinquent kid. No question about that. Still, for as much fun as Paris provided, I'd hardly call it anything like a vacation. One way or another, though, it was definitely something I'd never, ever tell my father.

Acknowledgements

The author wishes to thank Thaddeus Bower, Anne Dahlie, Elizabeth Dahlie, Eloise Flood, Kathrin Kollman, George Nicholson, and Paul Rodeen.